TIMESPINNERS

TIMESPINNERS

Luli Gray

HOUGHTON MIFFLIN COMPANY

BOSTON 2003

www.houghtonmifflinbooks.com

The text of this book is set in 12 point Dante.

Library of Congress Cataloging-in-Publication Data

Gray, Luli.
  The timespinners / Luli Gray.
    p. cm.
  Summary: A brother and sister go back in time to the Ice Age and meet
Neanderthals.
  ISBN 0-618-16412-X
  [1. Brothers and sisters--Fiction. 2. Twins--Fiction. 3.
Neanderthals--Fiction. 4. Time travel--Fiction.] I. Title.

PZ7.G7794 Ti 2003
[Fic]--dc21

                                        2002015323

Manufactured in the United States of America
QUM 10 9 8 7 6 5 4 3 2 1

For Mary Jane DiMassi,
who shared her vision,
and in loving memory of Richard Sax,
who nourished my dreams.

CHAPTER ONE

A T THE MOVIES THE MUSIC TELLS YOU WHEN TO be scared, but in real life there's no music. July 8 was just an ordinary day. Mim and Pa were in France for the summer, and Fig and I were staying with Aunt Bijou on the Upper East Side. When I woke up, I could smell the city through the open skylight above my bed, and I had kicked off the covers, which meant it was getting too hot to stay in town. New York is a great place in early summer but by July a cloud of stinky, dirty heat settles on the city and people get grouchy and mean. That's when we rent a car and take off for Maine, where even in August you need a sweater at night, and the ocean is so cold it makes you scream. We always stay at old Ms. McCulloch's cottage, and Fig and I explore the beaches while Bijou walks the hills with her sketch pad. We eat tons of clams and lobsters and take the jitney to whaling museums, baseball games, church bazaars, craft fairs, flea markets, food festivals, and used book stores. Last year our summer project was weird ice cream flavors. The winner was zucchini crunch, which was totally gross.

I stretched like Pie, hearing Bijou singing, "Yes! We have no bananas. We have no bananas today!" in the kitchen. We were leaving for Taylor's Cove on Monday, I had a new set of Prismacolors, a new Blue Avenger book to read, and a whole summer of adventures and ice cream to come. My brother was wrapped up like a mummy, as usual, with his cheek resting on the book he'd been reading when he fell asleep. It was *The Mysterious Stranger* by Mark Twain, the copy that belonged to Pa's older brother, Thad, who died in the Vietnam War. It's one of our favorite books. Fig rolled over and opened one eye.

"You shouldn't sleep on that book," I said. "It's old. You'll wreck it." My brother opened both eyes, crossed them, and stuck out his tongue. I couldn't help laughing. I guess I should tell you I'm Alice Cadwallader-Newton, only everyone calls me Allie. My brother is Thadeus Cadwallader-Newton, which is practically child abuse, so everyone calls him Fig. Fig Newton—get it? Ha ha. We're both ten and a half. We're fraternal twins. That means there were two eggs and two sperms. So really we're like a regular brother and sister except we were born at the same time. We're not at all like the Jessups, who are identical twins and really weird. They dress exactly alike, and no one can tell them apart. They could use that for doing all kinds of neat stuff, but they never do. They say the same things at the same time, and Fig says they're actually clones, which is pretty funny. He also says that we've known each other two hundred and eighty days longer than anyone else, and that is definitely true.

We've shared practically everything our whole lives. Only now Fig's clothes are all too short and tight for me. He says I probably have acromegaly, which is this disease that turns you into a giant. When we go back to Yellow House in the fall, Bijou is going to divide our room at her place and add a bathroom so I can have some privacy next summer. Sometimes I like the idea, and sometimes I don't.

I went into the bathroom, took off my T-shirt, and looked in the mirror. My hair is exactly like Fig's, or like Woody Woodpecker's according to Bijou; she wants me to grow it out or get a "decent" haircut. My body has turned into an alien blob with patches of red fuzz in embarrassing places. Ms. Hendley in Biology and Health class says I am "blooming into young womanhood," and Mim and Bijou keep telling me it's normal, whatever that means. I smelled my armpits and decided to skip the shower and just go swimming, so I covered up with a swimsuit and a pair of shorts and headed for the kitchen.

Bijou was arranging banana slices into smiley faces on three bowls of cereal. She looked up when I came in.

"Good morning, Allie Bee! I'll be in the studio all day. Shall we go to Dock's tonight to practice our lobster-eating technique?"

"We're going for a swim and then to the museum. We could meet you there," I said. I poured out three glasses of orange juice and sat down as Fig wandered in wearing nothing but a swimsuit.

"What's yellow and never rings?" he asked.

"I don't know, what *is* yellow and never rings?" asked Bijou.

"An unlisted banana!" He slid under the table, snorting with laughter, and Bijou ducked under too and tickled him. The snorts turned into shrieks and they both came up with bright red faces. Bijou rummaged through her shoulder bag and pulled out a sheet of paper.

"Here's my list for Taylor's Cove," she said, twisting up her hair and anchoring it with a barrette. "You two can add your own lists, and we'll pack tomorrow. If we leave at dawn on Monday, we'll be there that night."

I read the list while I ate: drawing pad, colored pencils, cat food, cat toys, butterscotch, hot sauce, bug spray, sunblock, water pistols, pressure cooker, chef's knife, saffron, inflatable shark, peppermill, *Moby Dick,* new Stephen King, map, kazoos.

"Brchshoo?" I asked and swallowed. "Bathing suits?"

"Oh, of course, put that down and flip-flops too," said Bijou, handing me a pen.

"The museum will be crowded today," I said, writing busily. "I wish all the people in New York would just disappear and go to—"

"IDAHO!" yelled Fig, which made me jump and knock over the milk.

"Oh, lovely," said Bijou, "Charming manners, I must say, little pigs."

I mopped up the mess with a handful of paper towels while Fig made pig noises. I ignored him. I'm the oldest by eleven minutes so I'm quite a lot more mature than my brother.

"Beej," said Fig, "exactly where will Mim and Pa be now?

4

Can you show us in the atlas? I want to see if I can find stuff from there at the museum."

"Well, let's see . . . Where's that letter?" Bijou walked into the living room and looked through her desk drawer. "Here it is," she said, waving a thin blue aerogram. "'Paris to Bordeaux by train, change for Souillac, then from there to St. Ann de Lavergne au Forêt by car with Dr. Wilde and her assistant.' That will be their base. Let's find it."

Fig pulled out the atlas, and we all sprawled on the rug looking for France, and then Paris (in big letters because it was the capital). There was Bordeaux, but we couldn't find Souillac or St. Ann de Lavergne au Forêt. "Too small," said Bijou. I thought it was funny that the smallest place had the longest name, and I wondered why the atlas people decided to color France orange. Germany is yellow and Spain is green. Why?

Bijou's cat, Pie, suddenly appeared from nowhere and sat down on southwestern France. All the cats I've ever known think books, magazines, and newspapers are for sitting on, especially when they are being read by humans.

"Pie, I can't *see*," I said, pushing her away.

"What wonderful names!" said Bijou, "Sauveterre, Parthenay, La Tremblade. . . . They sound like music, or beautiful colors."

"France is orange," said Fig, and Bijou rolled her eyes.

"You are very literal, bratlet."

"What does that mean?" I asked. I like new words.

"It means . . . oh . . . unimaginative. Well, you're not really that, cookie," she said, grinning at Fig.

"I want to look for Quigley," I said. "I almost saw him last summer, in the rhinoceros diorama."

"How can you almost see someone? You either see them or you don't," said Fig. "Besides, there's no such thing as ghosts."

"He's not a ghost, he's—"

Just then the phone rang, and Bijou reached for it, saying, "Early!" The grandfather clock in the corner of the living room said eight minutes past seven. Suddenly Bijou screamed. Fig grabbed my wrist and squeezed it way too tight. My aunt's voice was shaking.

"Oh god. Oh no. When? Yes, all right. Yes. Yes, I will. But when? Yes, all right, tomorrow." Bijou hung up and flopped into a chair as though her legs wouldn't hold her up, while Fig and I sat frozen, and waiting. At last Bijou looked up and spoke in a voice like a frog. "Oh, my babies, it's Mim."

That was it, the end of our summer, and from that moment everything changed. Sometimes I think if I could have turned the clock back just one minute, the phone wouldn't have rung and the bad, sad, mad time would never have come.

FIG'S NOTEBOOK

JULY 7

In *The Mysterious Stranger*, Mark Twain says, "Life itself is only a vision, a dream. Nothing exists save empty space . . . and you!" I don't see how that can be true. I know what's real and what isn't. Al likes MS because it's a fantasy, but I like it because it's realistic about how people act. It's supposed to take place in the 16th century but the people are just like they are now. They believe anything people say and don't ask questions. And they think the world works by magic, like the number thirteen is bad luck, or you can wish on stars. If you're going to be a scientist, which I am, you have to question everything. Mr. Garcia in A.P. Science says I am a thorn in his side, but I think he really likes it when I ask how do you *know* the earth is round? For sure, I mean?

Al is getting breasts and stuff. I wish she wouldn't.

CHAPTER TWO

A WEEK LATER, PA CAME HOME ON A MEDICAL transport plane with Mim strapped to a gurney. Now she's in Mt. Sinai Hospital in a room that looks out over Central Park, but she can't see it. She can't see it *yet* I mean. It was Pa who found her and pulled her out after the cave-in. She had a broken leg and lots of cuts and bruises; she was unconscious but alive. The doctors say she's not just unconscious, she's in a coma, and no one knows when she'll wake up. They say to talk to her, sing, read aloud—anything that might break through. She's all hooked up to tubes and machines that blink and hum, monitoring her heart and lungs and kidneys, and she looks so little.

The first time we went to the hospital Fig wouldn't speak. I didn't know what to say either, so I just babbled on and on about Maine (we didn't go) and the books I was reading and my friend Carly, who's going to be in a TV commercial. After a while the words felt large and furry, like tennis balls falling out of my mouth, so I went out to the hallway, where Fig sat on the floor with his back against the wall.

"You sounded totally lame," he said.

"I know."

"She's not there. That's not Mim."

I sat down and handed him a butter rum LifeSaver.

It's been a month now and Mim still hasn't woken up. The doctors say she's better. She's breathing on her own, and she's not as white as she was. Fig goes every day to tell her jokes and hold her hand when nobody's looking.

Bijou brings her sketch pad and draws while she talks about when she and Mim were kids. They looked exactly alike when they were little. Now that they're older, they don't. Bijou had a nose job for one thing, and her hair hangs halfway down her back. Mim cuts hers short, and it's curlier on the right side because she always runs her fingers through it when she's writing. They both have brown eyes. Fig and I have blue eyes like Pa, and we all have red hair.

Pa brings his laptop and talks to her about the book they were working on before the cave-in. It's called "Stones and Bones," and it's about the daily life of people in the Stone Age.

I help the nurse's aide massage Mim's arms and legs so the muscles won't atrophy, and I talk to her about what I'm going to be when I grow up. Before I'm a famous artist I'm going to be a famous actress, so I read to her from plays. When she was well, we used to do scenes together. Watching Mim be Joan of Arc or Lady Macbeth you'd never think she was an archaeologist or a mother.

Pa says he's sure she'll be well by September so we can go back to Yellow House as usual.

"This is just a detour," he said. We were in the American Museum of Natural History. It's huge and old and there are about a million corridors and staircases and enormous rooms with echoey ceilings. I had taken Pa to the little odds-and-ends room off the corridor, to look at the skeleton of Dreidel Boy. I wiped the glass case clean with my sleeve and read the label again: *#6327* AMNH 1938 *Homo neanderthalensis* C. 35,000 B.C. DORDOGNE, FR. I named him Dreidel Boy because the big bead in his hand reminds me of the dreidel Mim brought me from Israel. It's my best treasure. I looked around at the dusty cases of stuffed birds and broken pottery.

"I hope they don't throw him out with all this other junk," I said. "For a skeleton he has a really nice face."

"Oh, they won't," said Pa. "He's too valuable. You know what a detour is, don't you Allie? It's when you have to go around or climb over something to get back on your path. It's just temporary."

He was picking at the skin on the side of his thumb, and it looked kind of sore, so I took his hand.

"I'm sure she heard me when I was playing Ophelia from *Hamlet*," I said. "Her eyelids twitched."

"Yes!" said Pa. "I saw that too! She hears everything we say, I'm sure of it."

He grabbed me round the waist and danced us down the corridor singing,

"A capital ship for an ocean trip
Was the *Walloping Window Blind*.
No gale that blew dismayed her crew
Or troubled the captain's mind!"

We went to Gabriel's Café for an ice cream. I wasn't very hungry, so I picked at a dish of cherry sorbet and watched Pa eat two bites of his pistachio with hot fudge and moosh the rest into a lumpy brown puddle. We picked Fig up at the hospital and went home.

It was Pa's turn to make dinner. He always makes the same thing, chicken and rice with cream of mushroom soup. Fig and I set the table in the kitchen while Pa put the casserole together.

"We almost saw Quigley again," I said.

"There's no such thing as *almost* seeing," said Fig, "or ghosts either. I keep telling you."

"You don't know everything. Anyhow, Quigley is real, isn't he Pa?"

Pa mixed the canned soup with chicken broth and some yellow mustard. He likes mustard in or on practically everything.

"Quigley? Well, he *was* real, and he did disappear. I think it was around nineteen ten." He poured the soup over the chicken and rice, covered it with foil, and stuck it in the oven. Fig and I sat down to hear the story even though we'd heard it before.

"Hieronymous Quigley was one of the diorama painters, you know. He never was successful in the art world, but when Carl Akeley invented his special way of stuffing animal skins so they looked real, Quigley was just the man to paint the backgrounds for the displays. He was a kind of genius at painting animals and landscapes. They looked like you could just walk into the diorama and be right there in the middle of the African veldt, or the Brazilian rain forest, and people say that's just what happened. One minute he was standing there in front of the lynx diorama; the next, he was gone. Two guards were there; they saw him disappear." Pa licked the mustard off the spoon he was holding and threw it in the sink.

"How can you *see* someone disappear? That doesn't make sense," said Fig. "And what about the glass? He would have gotten cut, and anyhow, the dioramas aren't real."

"Well," said Pa, putting a basket of cherry tomatoes and a jar of pickled okra on the table, "they say he knew H. G. Wells, and maybe even Einstein. They had a lot of ideas about time and space and the nature of matter. Maybe Quigley picked up some pointers from them."

"Exactly!" I said. "It's like that old *Star Trek* episode, the one about the archway, where they jump into other times and places."

Fig rolled his eyes, which drives me totally up the wall—as if he's the only person in the world who knows anything.

"Excuse me?" he said. "That's called 'fiction.' You believe what you see on a dumb TV show? Hello?"

"I know it's fiction, *Thadeus*. Anyhow *Star Trek* isn't dumb; you hardly ever watch it, so how would you know?"

Pa and I both love *Star Trek*. Fig sometimes watches with us, but we like it better when he doesn't, because he makes fun of it the whole time. He mostly likes science programs and news and the Comedy Channel.

"It isn't dumb, is it, Pa?" Pa was picking at the label on the jar of okra and staring into space.

"What? No, no, Quigley wasn't at all dumb, though apparently he wasn't very good at managing money . . . they say he had a lot of creditors after him when he disappeared."

I was just starting to explain that we weren't talking about Quigley anymore when Bijou came in. She always goes to the hospital after she finishes at her studio in Brooklyn. I saw her before she came into the kitchen, and she looked like she'd been crying, but when she saw us all sitting there, she put on a big smile.

She hugged me and Fig and kissed Pa on the cheek. Then she turned on the oven (which Pa had forgotten) and got herself a glass of iced tea from the fridge.

"So!" she said, flopping down in a chair and reaching for the tomatoes.

"Pa and I saw Mim's eyelids twitch today, when we were talking to her. She's going to wake up really soon, I think." I said.

Bijou's smile sort of wobbled for a minute and then came back.

"Well, that's great, isn't it?"

Pa didn't say anything. I pulled on his arm and he jumped as though he'd forgotten I was there.

"It's a breakthrough, isn't it Pa?"

"Oh yes," he said. He took a deep breath and let it out with a *whoosh*. "Yellow House in the fall, back to normal anytime

13

now, I'm sure . . ." He got up suddenly and walked out of the kitchen. "Wash my hands," he said. "Right back."

We sat there without talking, smelling the chicken cooking and hearing the water running in the bathroom for a long, long time.

FIG'S NOTEBOOK

AUGUST 10

Mim is on oxygen, and she's hooked up to a blood pressure
monitor and an IV and a catheter. The machines are
pretty interesting. Dr. West says she doesn't have
head injuries so the coma is probably from shock.
Shock = circulatory failure. Her blood isn't going where
it's supposed to; even her nails and lips are pale.
Her face always gets red when she laughs, so if I could
make her laugh, it would help her circulation and
maybe help cure the coma. I tell her jokes from my book,
and I'm pretty sure her mouth twitched when I told her
the one about the duck. I told it to Dr. W. and he
laughed and said, "Laughter is the best medicine," and
rubbed my head, which means: You're just a kid, you
don't know anything.

I really hate that johnny they make her wear. It's all
open in the back, like it doesn't matter who sees her
without any clothes. I don't even know if she can hear me.

CHAPTER THREE

I WOKE UP SUDDENLY THIS MORNING AND IT TOOK ME a minute to realize I was in Bijou's apartment instead of home at Yellow House on the Hudson River. We've never been here at Christmastime before. I looked over at Fig, who was staring at me from his cocoon of blankets.

"Did you have it?" he asked.

"Yes. Did you?" He nodded. We've had the dream almost every night since July. We're in the cave, knowing what's going to happen, shouting a warning no one hears as the roof comes crashing down to trap Mim under tons of earth and stone. We claw and tear at the stones in slow motion, screaming and screaming. Sometimes Fig has it, sometimes it's me. Often we both do, and there's always Mim's hand sticking out from under the rubble and the choking smell of darkness.

Mim is still in her room at Mt. Sinai. She still can't see out the window, and we've watched Central Park go from green summer to yellow fall to white winter. Sometimes after her massage I stand there and look out, listening to Pa's voice. He sits there all day, every day, writing on a laptop and reading every word aloud, as though she can hear. Maybe she can; nobody knows. Pa often stays overnight, and when he does come home, he's way too polite, like he's a guest. When I hug him, his body is all angles, and when I try to talk to him, he seems to be somewhere else.

Bijou sits in the room holding Mim's hand or rubbing Jergen's lotion into her skin so it won't dry out. She doesn't talk much anymore. Once I heard her singing "I've Been Working on the Railroad." It sounded so strange without Mim singing harmony, and Bijou stopped when she saw me. When she's there, Pa sits in a chair by the window, writing. They hardly ever speak to each other now except to say necessary things like, "I'll pick them up around five." "Them" is Fig and me. Being called "them" when I'm right there makes me feel like a dog, or a bag of groceries. I know Bijou is trying to be a substitute mother, but I liked her better when she was just an aunt. I think it annoys her to have us around all the time. Sometimes she puts on this fake cheerful voice, and her smile looks like the lipstick mouths some ladies paint on when they have thin lips. Everything is different and horrible and Fig and I are hardly even friends. He says mean things to me all the time.

We've been going to the Chapman School since September and we both hate it. The principal, Dr. Chamblis, had all the teachers tell their classes about Mim, so now we're total freaks. Nobody wants to hang out with us; it's like comas are catching or something.

Today is Saturday, the first day of Christmas vacation. Bijou knocked on our door this morning and stuck her head in.

"What are your plans for today? After the hospital I thought we could rent a movie and order in, would you like that?"

"We're going to the museum. I don't care what we eat," I said. I can't help sounding rude. That's the way my voice comes out lately, and my face feels like it would break if I smiled.

I went into the kitchen, where Pa sat with a cup of cold coffee in front of him. Two slices of toast were still in the toaster. I buttered them and put them on a plate. "That's nice," he said when I told him we were out of marmalade and asked if he'd like honey instead. He ate two bites and got up to go to the hospital, though it was too early for visitors. "Keep up the good work!" he said and went into the front hall. I followed him and grabbed his hand.

"Pa! Don't say that, you never say that!" He opened the door and looked down as though he was surprised to see me attached to his other hand.

He patted me on the shoulder and said, "Fine, fine." The door closed behind him, and I flopped into a heap on the carpet as Fig came in from the kitchen.

"He's like a pod person from *Invasion of the Body Snatchers*," I said, wiping my eyes on my sleeve.

"He has posttraumatic stress disorder," said Fig. He stuffed his battered copy of *One Thousand Hilarious Jokes* into the pocket of his Great Men of Science sweatshirt.

"You can't keep telling her jokes," I said. "A person in a coma can't laugh."

"She loves jokes!" he said and burst into tears, which he hasn't done since he was seven and got his toe caught in a bike chain. Bijou came in dressed in a purple cape, pulling on a wool cap.

"Come on you guys, please don't squabble! Oh, Fig, what's wrong?" She reached out to hug him.

"Nothing," he said, pulling away.

Bijou didn't used to hug us all the time. I think she must've seen it on *Oprah* or something. I could tell she was going to try it on me, so I made my body stiff, and she was left standing there half bent over with her arms sticking out. She sighed and straightened up.

"I was thinking we might go to Rockefeller Center tomorrow, see the tree, maybe go skating, and have cocoa after? Would you like that?"

"It'll be full of tourists," I said. "Only tourists go to Rockefeller Center." Fig snickered, and I saw Bijou's mouth go crooked under the lipstick. I stood up, and she grabbed me.

"Oh, babies, I just don't know what to say to you! Everything I do is wrong! Can't you help me, please!"

"We're not babies—we're not *your* babies!" I twisted out of her arms.

"You're not our mother, anyhow," said Fig at the same time. Our words hung in the air, echoing in the suddenly silent room as Bijou's face turned white. After a minute she spoke in a low, tired voice.

"I know everything's changed. And Oliver is . . . well, he's very worried, we all are. But you two never used to be like this. We should try to help each other. We . . . look, it's a week till Christmas. Why don't you think about what you'd like to do, and we'll talk about it tonight, okay?"

"Fine," I said, wishing she would just go.

At last she did, and we went up for a swim in the glass-enclosed pool on the roof.

Nobody else was in the water. Old Mrs. Upshaw was stretched out on a chaise longue, wrapped in an afghan, and Ben the lifeguard sat all bunched up in his chair, wearing a hooded sweatshirt and drinking coffee from a Thermos. "Don't you guys drown, okay?" he said. "It's too cold to rescue you."

We ignored him and jumped in. The pool is best when there's no one else in it. The pool and sky are the same color, and when you swim between them, you don't know if you're swimming or flying, way above the city, away from everything. Sometimes I cry as I swim, and I think Fig does too. It doesn't matter; no one can see, and the tears just turn into part of the pool.

After, we put on sweats and windbreakers and walked across the park to the American Museum of Natural History. We go every chance we get. The first time we went we were only three. Mim and Pa left us to ride around all morning in a double stroller pushed by an archaeology student. I remember that because, when they came to pick us up in front of the African elephants, they seemed surprised to see us. Actually, they often seem surprised to see us after they've been away, as though they forget they have children.

Our favorite entrance is Central Park West, with the statue of Teddy Roosevelt on a horse at the foot of the stairs. A Native American man stands on one side of him and an African man stands on the other side. When I was little, I thought they all took turns on the horse. Behind the sculpture a broad flight of steps leads up to the Theodore Roosevelt Rotunda, which has a group of dinosaurs near the entrance. The skeleton of a barosaurus rears up to the ceiling, its baby stands behind it, and an allosaurus is about to attack them both. The sign says the barosaurus defended itself by falling on its enemies, which is just what this one seems about to do. The group was installed when we were little, and the first time we saw it, Pa said, "Ha! What nonsense! How do they think up this stuff anyway? Falling on its enemies for goshsakes . . . paleontologists!" Some little kids gathered around him, pulling away from their parents to listen. Pa ran his hands through his hair so it stuck up every which way, and his droopy red mustache flapped as he talked. He gestured at the dinosaur group, talking loudly about dinosaurs and paleontologists.

We sat under the barosaurus with Mim, waiting for Pa to finish. It's no use trying to stop him; it only makes him worse.

Even though Pa can be kind of embarrassing, it's neat having parents who can take us to the museum when it isn't crowded. Sometimes during the school year, when we're living in Yellow House, Mim and Pa let us cut school and come into the city on a Monday, when the museum's closed. We explore while Mim and Pa work in their office on the fourth floor, near the library. On Saturdays, of course, it's crowded so you have to stay away from the most popular places, like the Hall of Human Biology and Evolution, which has a lot of high-tech stuff that's pretty cool, if you can get to it through the huge mobs. Today we stood at the foot of the stairs, looking up at the entrance.

"Race you to the top!" I said and took off in a blinding burst of speed, like Jackie Joyner Kersee, while Fig shouted, "No fair!" behind me. When he got to the top, where I was waiting, his face was bright red. "That wasn't fair!" he said. "You should have said 'ready, set, go.' " I sighed.

"I know. You want reparation?"

I thought he'd ask for ice cream at Gabriel's but he only said, "It doesn't matter. But I get to pick what we see first."

We went through the revolving door and left our jackets in the cloakroom. A kind-looking lady at the information desk asked if she could help us.

"We want to see some things from Southwestern France, near Souillac, please," said Fig. The information lady took out a map of the museum and pointed at the Hall of European Mammals.

"That's on the ground floor, one level down, behind North American Mammals. It's due for renovation soon, but you can still go in," she said. "I'm not sure if there's anything specifically from France."

"Europe is a very large continent," said Fig. I thanked the lady and yanked him away from the desk.

"She's no use; she's totally clueless," said Fig. "We should have asked a scientist—a *French* scientist."

"That's ridiculous! That's just about the dumbest thing I ever heard! Why do you want to look at stuff from there anyway? That's just totally *sick!*" I didn't realize I was shouting till I felt a hand on my shoulder and heard a voice say, "Is there a problem here?" I turned around to see a tall man in blue sweats looking down at us. He smiled. "I might have known," he said. "You're Oliver Newton's children, aren't you?"

"Dr. Oliver and Dr. Miriam Cadwallader-Newton's, yes, we are," said Fig.

"And I'm Dr. Maldonado. I work here, and I know your parents. I'm so sorry about your mother." Fig picked at the picture of Galileo on his sweatshirt and nobody said anything for a minute.

Finally Dr. Maldonado said, "I'm an ornithologist, a scientist, though I'm not French. Do you think I might be able to help you?"

Fig pulled a grubby piece of paper from his pocket. It was the map he had copied from the atlas months before, on the day of the terrible phone call.

"We wanted to see if there was any stuff from there," he said.

"Artifacts, not stuff," I said. "And I don't want to, it was *your* dumb idea."

"Oh, we have both," said Dr. Maldonado. "Artifacts and stuff, dumb and smart, animals and birds, of course. Let's see now . . ." He peered at the map. "The lynx and the foxes are from France, I believe. I was examining them only this morning, as it happens."

He led us to an elevator and showed us where to go. "Let me know if there's anything I can do to help," he said as the elevator doors opened.

Grownups are always saying that. It doesn't mean anything. The only thing that would help would be if they could bring Mim back, and they can't.

FIG'S NOTEBOOK

DECEMBER 19

I'm not going to be a doctor when I grow up. They don't know much. They just make guesses. Mim is the same, only thinner. Nurse Beverly, who is her main daytime nurse, says there's everything in the IV she needs, but it's not the same as food. Mim's favorite food is pulled pork barbecue, like they have in North Carolina where her and Beej's Uncle Donald is. I only met him once. He's a doctor but he's really old—seventy-five. He said you should never hold in farts and belches because they poison your system. Bijou says that is absolutely not true. Uncle Donald can belch whenever he wants to, and so can I.

Pa has gotten totally weird. He hardly even talks. Beej is okay but kind of annoying. I think Al has PMS. She is really mean.

I hate it here.

CHAPTER FOUR

W E WERE THE ONLY PEOPLE ON THE SLOW, OLD
elevator. I thought about how white Bijou's face
was when she left, and wished I could take back what I said.

"Skating would be fun, I bet," said Fig. "And cocoa." I
scowled at him.

"Then why didn't you say something, if you think Rockefeller Center is so great."

"You were mean," said Fig.

"So were you. You said she's not our mother."

"Well, she's not." The elevator doors opened and two
grownups with two little boys got on. They were all wearing
down coats and carrying cameras, and they looked hot and
sort of frantic. I pushed the button to hold the door open.

"You can check your coats on the next floor up," I said. The
lady smiled and nodded as the doors closed.

"I don't think they understand English," said Fig after we
got off the elevator. "Or they would've said thank you."

"Maybe they were just rude."

"Maybe they were rude *and* foreign," he said.

There was hardly anyone else on the ground floor except for some people around the gift shop. We hurried through North American Mammals, turned right, then left, and walked down a short corridor. I wanted to stop and look at Dreidel Boy but Fig hurried on.

"You owe me," he said over his shoulder. "We have to see what *I* want." I made a face at his back and followed him down the hall, dragging my feet. I didn't even want to think about the place where Mim got hurt. I was afraid seeing things from there might be bad luck.

I have to admit the Hall of European Mammals is pretty cool. I don't think we'd ever explored it before. It's easy to miss. If you're in the odds-and-ends room where Dreidel Boy is, you naturally walk straight on into North American Mammals. Instead Fig followed Dr. Maldonado's directions and turned left at the case full of arrowheads. A low archway leads into an alcove that opens out into a big oval room with dioramas set into the walls. If you've never been to a really good museum, you might not know how real-looking dioramas can be. The animals and birds look almost alive behind the glass, even though they were killed a long time ago and are kind of moth-eaten. Some dioramas seem more real than others. Whether it's the way they're painted or just a trick of the light, some of the scenes are so lifelike that the animals look like they're about to roar or run or fly away. If you stand about twenty feet from the glass, the trees and bushes lose their dead look and go all shiny—you can almost smell them. We walked around the whole room and decided the lynx diorama was the realest. A big cat sits under the trees, and her two kittens are curled up in a pile of leaves nearby. The mother cat is four times as big as Pie, with tufted ears and huge, furry feet. The lynxes are hard to see at first because their speckled fur blends into the background. The big one is snarling so you can see its long, sharp teeth. We stepped back to just the right distance and looked again. The sky arched up, a few birds were in the distance, and the light filtered down through the leaves in dusty gold streaks. The cats looked strong and alive, ready to pounce or run away through the trees.

I wondered whether there still were any lynxes in St. Ann de Lavergne au Forêt and whether Mim and Pa had seen them. The gold letters on the frame said, *Lynx lynx,* and in smaller black letters below, COLLECTED BY JOBE EXPEDITION 1913, EXTREMELY RARE. Off to one side, even smaller letters said, BACKGROUND BY H. QUIGLEY. Quigley!

"Hey Fig!" I said. "The lynx group! That's where Pa said Quigley disappeared! Remember? He . . ."

"Will you please shut up about Quigley? I'm trying to study this so I can tell Mim. It might make her wake up."

He was copying the sign that listed all the plants and animals into his pocket notebook. I scowled at him, sending poison thought-rays through his sweatshirt, and stepped back from the diorama. "Hey, Figgy-Wiggy," I said. "Oh, Thadeus, guess what? I'm going into the diorama just like Quigley!" He ignored me.

I put my arms out and spun around till I got dizzy. I ended facing the diorama and stared for a minute, trying to focus.

"Fig, look! When you spin and stop, it gets totally real. I saw it move!"

He looked up from his notebook and walked over to where I was standing.

"It's just because you're dizzy," he said. "It makes you see things that aren't real, like when people are drunk."

"Maybe when people are drunk they see things that are really there only the not-drunk people can't see them." (I don't actually believe this. I said it to drive my brother up the wall.) Fig rolled his eyes and I began to spin slowly, chanting, "Quigley, Quigley, Quigleee!"

Fig's face turned red, and I knew he was trying not to laugh. After a minute he put his arms out too and began to turn. The room blurred; the dioramas rushed past as we spun faster and faster. We both stopped suddenly, facing the lynx group, and the room seemed to go on spinning as I staggered toward the diorama.

"Here I come, ready or not!" I said and jumped, holding both hands out to catch myself against the glass. But instead of the hard surface I expected, my fingers slid into a soft, cool dampness, and I screamed, pulling back and falling against my brother.

"Your hand went right through," he said, staring. He took my hand and turned it over, examining it like a doctor.

"It's cold. Does it hurt?" I shook my head.

"It just felt kind of wet and cold, like fog." I wiggled my fingers to see if they were okay. "Fig, that must be what happened to—"

"Quigley," he said. "So it is true! He must have gone into

the diorama." He got up and touched the glass with the tip of one finger.

"It's hard again," he said.

"Maybe we imagined it."

The lynxes looked stuffed and dusty and dead.

"I don't imagine things. Let's spin and see if it happens again." I didn't really want to; it felt creepy. But I wasn't going to let Fig think I was chicken. We stood back from the diorama and began to spin. Sure enough, the scene behind the glass changed and came alive, the wild cats strong and sleek and dangerous.

"Allie, let's go through," said Fig, spinning more slowly.

"I don't . . ." I started to say, then I remembered what waited for us at home, and I just wanted to be somewhere, anywhere else.

"Yes!" I said. "Let's go," and we leapt at the glass together with our arms stretched out and our heads down like divers. A cool gray fog enveloped us, swirling around us as we tumbled through it to land with a bump, all in a heap on a cushion of moss.

We untangled ourselves, stood up, and looked around. The trees grew so thickly that the light looked green, and in the distance a herd of deer stood grazing in a meadow full of sunlight. Behind us the Hall of European Mammals was fuzzy and out of focus. We smelled earth and wind instead of stuffy museum air, and now that we had stopped screaming we could hear birds and small creatures moving through the forest.

"We're *inside* the diorama," I whispered. We looked back

at the museum just as a guard in a blue uniform strolled into the hall. Fig yelled, "Hey!" But the guard leaned against the wall beside the doorway looking at his watch, and I knew he couldn't see or hear us.

"How do we go back?" I asked. We felt all around the grayness to find an opening, but the soft misty surface had turned hard as stone, and as we stepped back the Hall of European Mammals vanished. Where it had been was forest and more forest, cool, green, and so quiet I could hear my own heartbeat.

"We're stuck," said Fig. I nodded. We shouted for the guard until we were hoarse, hoping the museum would reappear. At last we stopped.

"All the dioramas have a back wall with a door," said Fig. "We have to find it, that's all." He didn't sound very sure of himself.

"Right," I said. "We'll find the door." We looked around at all the trees and the deer in the distance. It was cold in the forest and the meadow looked warm and sunny, so after a while we turned and walked, slowly, deeper into the diorama.

FIG'S NOTEBOOK

DECEMBER 20

SIGN: *Lynx lynx* Collected by Jobe Expedition 1913.
Extremely rare. Background by H. Quigley.

TREES	SHRUBS	ANIMALS	FLOWERS
oak	hawthorn	lynx (3)	woodbine
beech	elder	squirrel	crowsfoot
birch		vole	periwinkle

BIRDS	INSECTS
greenish warbler	horsefly
redstart	ladybird beetle
nuthatch	swallowtail butterfly
tree sparrow	honeybee

CHAPTER FIVE

W HEN WE GOT TO THE EDGE OF THE FOREST,
we saw a group of tents on the far side of the clearing. An antique car was parked nearby, and several people were moving around the camp. Fig and I peeked out from behind a tree. The people in the camp were wearing khaki clothing, boots, and hats like hunters on an African safari, but we couldn't see their faces or tell what they were doing.

"This diorama's in France," said Fig. "They're campers, I bet."

"It's safe then. French people aren't dangerous."

"They were during the French Revolution and the Terror," said Fig. "They chopped everyone's head off."

This was too ridiculous to even answer, so I began walking toward the tents. Fig followed me. "No guillotine," he said.

As we got close, one of the men saw us and called out to the others in words I knew were French. A woman stepped forward. She had a long braid down her back and she wore khaki-colored culottes and boots. She seemed to be the leader because she stepped forward and said,

"Qui êtes-vous? Qu'est-ce-que vous faites ici, dans le forêt? Ou sont vos parents?"

I tried to remember the French we learned three years ago, when we were in Boulogne with our parents. It was just before Mim decided we needed a more normal life, so we only stayed two months before we went back to Yellow House and school. I thought maybe if I spoke very slowly she might understand.

"Je suis Alice Cadwallader-Newton," I said. "This is *mon frère,* Fig. We came through the diorama. *Nos parents* are not here."

"Americans!" said the woman. "What are you doing here, and where are your parents?"

"She told you," said Fig, "we came through the diorama."

"What diorama? What on earth do you mean?" she asked.

"Our parents are in New York. We came from the museum." The woman stared at us, pinching her lower lip between her thumb and forefinger and scowling.

"Am I to understand that your parents allowed you to travel all the way from New York with some sort of museum society dressed in such inappropriate . . . well, it's outrageous, and . . . André, *s'il vous plait!"* The man who had shouted came up to her, and they talked in French.

That's when I noticed the calendar nailed to a tree nearby. It showed a picture of a cat sitting on a crate of asparagus and the letters underneath said, MAY 1913. I pinched Fig's arm, and we stared at those numbers while the woman talked with André. After a while he nodded and ducked into one of the tents. The woman turned back to us and said, "Don't worry, kiddies, there's a telephone in the town. André will motor over in the morning and call the authorities in Paris. They'll reach your parents soon enough, if you're telling the truth. They must be very irresponsible people." Fig and I started to protest but she stopped us with a wave of her hand.

"Now don't fuss! Let's not have any nonsense. I expect you'd better have something to eat and something warm to wear. The Dordogne can be chilly in May. And by the way, I am Mary Jobe."

Something she said sounded familiar. It's something orange that keeps slipping away just as my mind touches it.

We followed Mary Jobe into the largest tent and put on the heavy wool shirts she gave us. She went out and brought back mugs of sweet, milky coffee, a box of crackers, and a tin of sardines. Even though it was a strange sort of lunch it tasted good and so did the coffee. I'm pretty sure it wasn't decaf, which is all we're allowed at home.

Mary Jobe sat on a campstool, watching us eat. "I suppose we'll have to find you some blankets for tonight," she said.

"I'm sorry," I said. "We didn't mean to barge in, it's just, well, we don't know where we are."

"Oh, it's easy enough to get lost in this forest, happens all the time, though your museum people should have been more careful. I imagine they're organizing a search party; perhaps they'll show up before nightfall. I certainly hope so. This is a hunting expedition and no place for children."

She seemed to think we were with some sort of tourist organization or school. We didn't think we could explain it, so we didn't even try. Someone called from outside and Ms. Jobe told us to stay where we were as she went out through the flap.

Fig and I sat on the camp bed and discussed our situation. We figured we had the night and maybe half the next day before André got back with no report on our parents.

"If it's really 1913, Mim and Pa aren't even born," I said, "Even *their* parents aren't born yet."

That's all we knew. It was May of 1913, and we were somewhere in France called the Dordogne. I wasn't worried about the France part of it. You can always get from one place to another, and we'd been to France before. It was the date that scared me. Then I remembered why I thought of something orange when Mary Jobe said we were in the Dordogne.

"The atlas!" I said. "France was orange, and the Dordogne is where the cave was where Mim got hurt!"

Fig gulped. "Ninety years. Ninety years *before* she got hurt."

We thought about that for a while, and I watched Fig chew on the cuticle of his left thumb the way he does when he's scared. I've read a lot of science fiction stories about time travel and they gave me an idea.

"Fig, maybe if we change the past, the cave-in won't happen!"

"If we change the wrong thing, we might never be born," he said.

It's true that in some of the time travel stories people change just one thing about the past and it totally changes the future. Like, they make George Washington forget his hat on his way to the Battle of Monmouth. Then he catches a cold that turns into pneumonia and he dies and the Americans lose the revolution, and there's never any United States of America at all and the time traveler disappears—*POOF!*—like a blown-out candle.

"Anyhow those are just stories, not science," said Fig.

"But what if they're possible?" I asked. "We should try it at least, and then go back to where the diorama was. Maybe that would help us get back."

Fig wanted to stay and see the hunting and then go back.

"I don't want to see killing, just hunting."

"It's the same thing," I said. He said it wasn't.

Finally I said, "Don't you see we have to make sure we *can* get back!"

"Of course we can, we just spin like before." He stood up and began to spin, arms out. Nothing happened. We didn't say anything for several minutes.

"I don't think we're even *in* the diorama anymore. And there's a war coming soon," Fig said. "France and Germany, I think." I took a deep breath, in through the nose and out through the mouth. Mim says that's a good way to calm down if you're scared or nervous, so I did it a couple more times.

"Maybe the diorama's a gate through time and we have to be closer to where we came in for it to work," I said. "But I don't want to meet any Nazis, and I don't want to see things killed!"

Fig was inspecting a rifle that was leaning against the wall of the tent.

"There's no such thing as a gate through time. Anyhow, Nazis were a different war," he said, reaching to pick it up.

"Don't touch it! It might go off," I said. He came back to the bed and sat down.

"Not from just touching it won't," he said. I was about to argue when Mary Jobe came back, looking annoyed. She told us André couldn't get the "automobile" to start and was taking the engine apart to see if he could fix it. "So you'll just have to stay for the time being. We'll keep trying." She looked at us as though she were sizing us up.

"Do you kiddies think you can do as you're told and not get in the way on a hunting trip?" she asked.

Fig said, "We won't get in the way, and we're not kiddies."

Mary Jobe raised her eyebrows. "Well! We'll see about that. We'll be out all day, and it's hard walking. Can you keep up?"

"We've gone on hikes with our parents, all day for weeks and weeks, carrying packs too," I said.

"*Hmph!*" said Ms. Jobe. "Well, I hope so, because we can't just leave you here on your own." She told us where the latrine was, a hole in the ground with a couple of boards over it—very splintery boards, as I soon found out. We washed our hands in a basin of water from a nearby spring.

"That wasn't true," said Fig, turning the soap around in his hands to make lather. "We've only ever done two nights, and the packs just had water and raisins in them."

"She was rude," I said. "She doesn't like us."

Mary Jobe introduced us to the other members of the expedition. André, who speaks almost no English, is their guide.

He has a humongous mustache, and he smiles a lot. Gordon is an English zoologist and his job is to make drawings and photographs of the animals they shoot. He showed us his notebook. The drawings included deer, hares, birds, and on the last page, a group of lynxes. "Oh!" I cried, "Have you killed those poor cats? That's so cruel!" He said they hadn't shot anything yet except rabbits "for the pot," and he does the drawings by sitting very still in the forest until the creatures stop being scared of him. They were really good drawings. When I try to draw animals, they look goofy, like toys. Gordon said the lynxes are hard to draw because they're so wary; he has to do them from a distance. "We'll go after them tomorrow," he said, putting away his pencils.

Fig asked him if "go after" meant hunting, and he said yes, of course. That's when I got my idea.

I thought that if we changed something in this time, it might change the future so Mim wouldn't get hurt. And maybe if it was a good deed, nothing bad would happen, like our not being born. According to the sign on the diorama it was the Jobe Expedition that shot the lynxes, so saving them would be a good deed for sure.

That evening we sat around the fire and ate rabbit stew and a kind of tough flatbread baked in the coals. Gerard, who is the driver and also the best shot, did the cooking, and we helped him to wash up afterwards with water and sand for scrubbing the pot. He spoke English quite well and said "bully!" and "swell!" when he was pleased and "thunderation!" when he wasn't. Mary Jobe is the only mean one. She acts like she'll lose her temper any minute, and Fig and I decided she doesn't like children at all.

After supper Mary Jobe handed us a couple of blankets and told us to roll ourselves up and sleep on the floor. She took off her boots, culottes, shirt, and jacket, and climbed into a camp bed wearing long underwear and wool socks.

"Put out that lantern. We want an early start," she said.

Fig and I didn't have much time to talk about my idea, and Mary Jobe wasn't at all friendly, but Pa says you have to do the right thing even if it's hard.

"Ms. Jobe," I began.

"What is it?" she asked, all wrapped up in the bed with her back to us.

I took a deep breath and said it all in a rush. "We came here from the American Museum of Natural History in New York by some kind of time travel from the year 2003 and here our parents aren't even born yet!"

Mary Jobe sat up in bed scowling. "Look, kiddies," she said, "we have a long day tomorrow, and I don't have time for silly stories, so just go off to sleep, will you!" As she started to lie down I leaned over and grabbed her arm.

"It's true, Ms. Jobe!" She was so grouchy I didn't know what to do, but Fig did. He pulled a handful of change out of his pocket and dumped it in her lap. She jumped, and the coins scattered over the blanket: quarters, dimes, nickels, and two pennies. "Look!" he cried. "Please, Ms. Jobe, look at the dates!" She looked more closely, picking them up one by one. She held a quarter between her thumb and forefinger as she ran her eyes over us like a policeman looking for evidence.

"What kind of watch is that?" she asked, staring at Fig's wrist.

"Digital," he said, taking it off to show her. She turned it over in her hands.

"Digital! What do you mean?"

Fig tried to explain about quartz crystals and microchips, and he drew a diagram in his notebook, but I don't think Ms. Jobe understood it any better than I do. I told her about jumping into the diorama, and she listened with her whole body, like Mim does, with the watch in one hand and the quarter in the other. "The twenty-first century," she said. "Is it possible?" All at once her whole face lit up with a wonderful smile.

"Time travel!" she said, "Just like Mr. Wells. Tell me everything!"

Fig and I told her as much as we could think of: space travel, VCRs, computers. Mary Jobe only seemed interested in the space travel.

"Moving pictures, typewriting machines, aeroplanes—we have those," she said. "If you're telling the truth, there must be more."

"Endangered species," I said. "Lots of animals are endangered or extinct because of human overpopulation and habitat destruction and deforestation. And hunting."

"*Hmph!* Big words for a kid," said Mary Jobe. "I'm not surprised. The passenger pigeon is gone, or nearly so, and the buffalo too. That's why I'm collecting these creatures, so there will at least be a record of them in museums. There aren't many lynx left in Europe."

"Then you shouldn't shoot them!" I said.

"If *I* shoot them, they'll go into a museum, and people in your time will know they existed. Otherwise a hunter will shoot them, or they'll just die and disappear altogether. I do it for Science."

That's exactly what Fig said when he put the angelfish in the goldfish tank in second grade to see what would happen. The next day there was just one really fat angelfish and no goldfish at all. Ms. Binkley was mad, but I knew Fig didn't mean any harm. "I did it for Science," he said, and then he cried. Of course the goldfish were still dead.

We couldn't convince Ms. Jobe to spare the lynxes no matter how much we argued. Finally she told us to go to sleep, put out the lantern, and rolled herself up in the bedcovers. Then, in a storm of blankets, pillows, and long brown hair, she got up, hustled us into the bed, and lay down on the floor in a cocoon of bedding. "Blasted brats!" she said. When we stopped giggling, we curled up back to back and fell asleep.

FIG'S NOTEBOOK

DECEMBER 21

I don't get why I didn't go back to our own time when I spun. There's a key to it, I know. If I could just figure it out ... I've read some time travel stories but they were just made up. Pa says time travel is probably not possible. This is definitely real, though, so I guess he's wrong. I keep thinking about what's happening at home because of our changing things in this time. Just our being here must be changing the future. I don't think Allie understands how dangerous it is.

HOW A QUARTZ WATCH WORKS

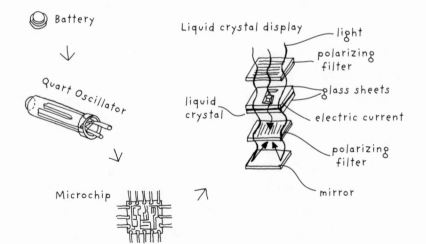

Battery

Quart Oscillator

Microchip

Liquid crystal display

liquid crystal

light

polarizing filter

glass sheets

electric current

polarizing filter

mirror

CHAPTER SIX

EARLY THE NEXT MORNING MS. JOBE SHOOK US awake and handed us two pairs of khaki pants and two pieces of rope. "Your legs will get scratched to pieces in those thin drawers. Put these on," she said. We put the pants on over our sweats, but they were still way too big, so we rolled up the legs and used the ropes for belts. Outside everyone was drinking coffee and eating slabs of bread with honey. Gerard handed us mugs of coffee and added condensed milk. " 'Ere's mud in your eyes, keeds," he said, grinning. Even though it did taste sort of muddy, it was hot and sweet, and it was all there was.

André slid out from under the car, cursing and covered with grease. He spoke to Mary Jobe, pointing at Fig and me, and they argued for a while. Then he shrugged, threw up his hands, and disappeared into his tent. When he came out, he was carrying a gun. *"Allons y, alors,"* he said and walked off into the forest. We all followed. My brother and I walked with Gerard, who is the friendliest of the grownups. We walked quite slowly because Ms. Jobe wanted everyone to make as little noise as possible, so it wasn't hard to keep up. Besides André, Mary Jobe and Gerard carried guns too. Gordon carried his notebook and pencils in a knapsack and had a big old-fashioned camera he called a Kodak slung over his shoulder on a leather strap.

"I wish we had our hiking boots," said Fig. So did I. Sneakers are not the best thing for walking through a forest, and I was glad Ms. Jobe made us wear the khaki pants. Brambles kept catching at our legs, and it was cold under the trees.

Late in the morning, when I felt like we'd been walking for days, André raised his hand, and we stopped. He put a finger to his lips and pointed. At first I could see only trees and bushes. Then, through the speckly pattern of light and shade I saw the lynxes fifty feet away. Two cubs pounced and wrestled, climbing all over their mother, who was stretched out on her back, basking in the sun with a paw over her nose, swatting the little ones when they got too rough.

We all watched, scarcely breathing. Then André raised the gun to his shoulder and took aim. Gerard squinted down the barrel of his weapon and looked at Mary Jobe, ready to fire on her signal. She lifted her own gun off the crook of her arm. Streaks of sun filtered down through the pines, and all the forest seemed to be waiting. I could hear the kittens squealing. Just as I opened my mouth to scream, Ms. Jobe lowered her gun. André raised his eyebrows and gestured toward the cats with his rifle. "Don't shoot. Put down your guns," said Ms. Jobe under her breath. André made an exasperated sound through his teeth and uncocked his rifle, while Gerard shook his head and rubbed his hair into a tangle, which seemed to be his way of expressing confusion. Ms. Jobe told Gordon to get a photograph of the cats and beckoned to the rest of us to follow her. We walked off as quietly as we had come, and when I looked back, I saw Gordon sit down cautiously on a log, aiming his camera at the cats, who still hadn't noticed him.

We came to a clearing in the forest, and Ms. Jobe ordered a rest. Gerard pulled out a packet of sandwiches made of bread and bars of dark chocolate and a bottle of wine. Mary Jobe led us to a tree a little way from the men and sat chewing on her sandwich. I touched her arm.

"Thank you for not shooting those cats, Ms. Jobe."

She looked at my hand as though it were a blob of ketchup on her sleeve.

"I don't know why I stopped it," she said. "Even if your story is true, I know I'm right. Those cats won't live forever no matter what I do, and they'll be extinct in your time anyway. I just couldn't do it."

I didn't know what to say. We sat there for a long time, watching the birds and squirrels and rabbits and eating bread and chocolate. It was pretty good once you got used to it.

At last Ms. Jobe stood up and stretched, and we stood up too. By this time Gordon had caught up and was eating his lunch with André and Gerard, who lay on their backs smoking smelly brown cigarettes.

"I got a good one of the cats, Mary," said Gordon. "Then

they got spooked and ran away. I'll go by myself tomorrow and try again."

"Splendid, Gordon; thank you. You three go on back to camp, we'll join you in a while."

The men stood up, shouldered their knapsacks, and walked off, smoking and talking now that there was no reason to be silent.

When they were out of sight, Ms. Jobe said, "Do you remember where you came in, more or less? Were there any landmarks?"

Fig and I thought for a moment and told her about the enormous oak tree. She shook her head. The forest was full of oak trees and many of them were enormous.

"The clearing was ahead of us, a long way. We could just see your tents," said Fig.

I shut my eyes and tried to see it in my mind. "The tree had a limb broken off on one side and I tripped over a huge root sticking out of the ground. When we saw your camp, the car was on the left."

"Good!" she said, "I think I can find it." She marched off as though she knew exactly where she was going, and after a long walk we came to the edge of the clearing opposite the camp. We could see the men moving around the tents in the distance and the car just like I said, on the left.

"This is it, near here," I said excitedly. Sure enough, there was the oak tree.

"Now where?" asked Ms. Jobe.

It seemed like ages since we came through the forest

though it had only been the day before. Even though I was pretty sure we had walked in a straight line, I know how easy it is to get confused in the woods.

"The sun!" said Fig. "It was on our left, I remember; it felt warm on my arm."

"Splendid!" said Ms. Jobe, and we set off again. After about twenty minutes she stopped and asked if we were near the entrance. We couldn't tell her. It was just trees everywhere and no sign of the square frame of the diorama.

"You'll just have to try," said Ms. Jobe. Fig and I looked at each other and knew she was right. We stepped away, put our arms out, and began to spin. We spun slowly at first, then faster and faster, till the forest blurred into a green fog. The green fog turned to gray mist. "It's working!" cried Fig. It *was* working. We were falling through cool, swirling mist—we were going home! Just as before we landed with a bump and sat up to look around.

We were still in the forest, and it had gotten much colder. There were patches of snow on the ground, and the trees were bare except for green buds at the tips of the branches.

"We're still here," said Fig. I nodded and pulled up the hood of my sweatshirt. We began walking, hoping to find the clearing as before with Mary Jobe's nice grumpy face scowling at us and the smell of Gerard's bread baking in the coals. After a while Fig said, "It's not *where* we are, it's *when*. When are we?"

I looked around. There was no smell of smoke; there were only the ordinary sounds of a forest: the rustle of branches in the wind, a bird call now and then. At last we saw an opening in the trees and walked toward it, wanting to get out of the shade and into the sunshine. The path was narrow so we went single file with me in front, and as I walked I noticed some large, dark shapes far away across the meadow. I thought they were boulders at first, and then I saw they were moving. They were much too big for deer, and I couldn't figure out what they were. They were almost like . . . I stopped suddenly, so Fig bumped into me. Then he bumped me again on purpose to get me back, but I didn't care because I was staring as hard as I could with a big, goofy grin wrapping itself right around my head. I couldn't even talk; all I could do was bounce up and down and point till Fig saw what I was staring at. The huge creatures marched over the meadow, dark against the sky, shaggy, amazing, impossibly and absolutely real: *MAMMOTHS!*

We stared with our eyes bugged out and our mouths open. I counted twelve of them including three babies; one enormous mammoth had curved tusks that nearly crossed at the tips. We must have been downwind of them because they didn't seem to notice us and went on grazing, the babies galloping around under their legs.

Suddenly Fig flopped to the ground. I was surprised to see that his face had turned pale green as though he were about to throw up.

"They're herbivores," I said. "They won't hurt us."

Fig shook his head, staring at the herd.

"Don't you get it?" he said. "They're mammoths—woolly mammoths! That's why it's so cold; we've gone *back* again. We're in the Ice Age!"

I stared at the mammoths that had seemed so wonderful a

minute ago. The breeze blew through my clothes, and I shivered. I hunkered down and chewed on the inside of my cheeks so I wouldn't cry. After a while Fig stood up.

"It's going to get colder when the sun sets. We better find some kind of shelter," he said.

"We have to try again," I said. "We have to get home!" My voice was hoarse and my teeth were chattering.

"Yeah, but it's no good if we freeze to death before we have a chance to try," said Fig. "Come on." We began walking across the clearing, getting closer and closer to the mammoths. The leader raised her head, smelling us or hearing our footsteps. She watched us for a moment, swaying on her tree trunk legs, and went back to eating. I guess she knew she could crush us into jam with one foot.

The mammoths moved slowly over the meadow, and even though I was scared I couldn't help being excited too. Nobody for thousands of years, nobody in our time has ever seen a live mammoth! I began swinging my arms like a soldier for courage and to keep warm. Fig began marching, too, and singing. We sang one marching song after another: "Marching to Pretoria," "Waltzing Matilda," "Eatin' Goober Peas," and "This Old Man."

"This old man, he played one,
   He played knick-knack on my thumb;
   With a knick-knack paddywhack, give a dog a bone,
   This old man came rolling home."

We had just gotten to "he played eight" when Fig grabbed my arm.

"Hush! Someone's there; I heard it." We looked all around. There was no one in sight and no sound but the wind. Beyond the meadow the forest rose up into a shallow slope with snowy hills beyond, and as we reached the top Fig stopped and pointed. "Look!" he said. "That looks like a cave—there, in those rocks." I saw it too, a dark hole in the side of a ridge, half hidden by bushes. I thought about cave bears and the eyeless, pale things that live in the dark, and about Mim crushed under the rocks.

"Fig, I can't!" He took both my hands and looked me in the eye.

"We have to, Al. If we don't, we'll freeze to death. We'll die." His hands were warm on mine, and he was squeezing them too hard.

"Ow! Okay, I'll go, but I'm not going all the way in." We walked on.

The sun sank low and the air grew colder. My cheeks burned and the wind stung my eyes and made my nose run. The cave seemed to get no closer. I heard my stomach growling and thought about hot cocoa with marshmallows melting slowly into the steamy chocolate. When Fig stumbled, I grabbed him, and we walked hand in hand toward the distant ridge with the Ice Age wind hissing around us.

FIG'S NOTEBOOK

DECEMBER 22

The calendar says May, but it's pretty cold here at night. I don't think Ms. Jobe understands my watch diagram but she's trying to help us, or maybe she's just trying to get rid of us. I'd really like to learn how to shoot a gun. Pa doesn't have one at home but he knows how to shoot and so does Mim. They should've taken me with them instead of leaving me in New York. I probably could have saved Mim from the cave-in because I pay attention way better than Pa.

I didn't have the nightmare last night, neither did Al. Maybe if Ms. Jobe helps us get back to our time, Mim will be okay. I wonder if praying works even if you don't believe in it.

CHAPTER SEVEN

THE SUN SET BEHIND THE HILLS, STAINING THE
snow blood-red. The sky turned dark blue, and the
moon rose over the pines as we kept on walking, too hungry
and tired to talk. Half blinded by the wind, we plodded forward step by step toward the cave we couldn't even see. All we
could see was the ridge, shining in the moonlight, and all I
could feel was Fig's hand in mine as we staggered on.

Night creatures began to move around us in the darkness.
Red eyes glowed through the trees, and invisible things rus-
tled. I thought about the saber-toothed cats, dire wolves, cave
bears, and giant hyenas I had seen in the museum.

We stopped to catch our breath. Fig looked like an old
man, hunched over with his head hanging down. I looked up
at Venus, the evening star, shining through the darkness, and
thought I heard Mim's voice,

"Star light, star bright

First star I see tonight,

I wish I may, I wish I might

Have the wish I wish tonight."

I saw we had come almost to the ridge and I tugged at my brother's hand. "Fig!" I cried. "Fig, we're almost there!"

He raised his head to look and then we started walking again, toward the shine.

"Almost there," I said, "almost . . . *NOOO!*" The beast came out of nowhere, clawing, crushing, snarling, hot breath stinking of blood as we screamed and fought to keep its teeth from our throats.

"Mee Low!" The shout yanked the beast back like a leash, leaving us breathless and staring at the strange creature who loomed over us holding a torch, his face hideous in the flickering light. He had a big blobby nose, almost no chin, and heavy ridges over eyes as blue as ours. His feet were bare, and he wore a long tunic made of furry animal skins. Though he was no taller than Fig he was much heavier, and the look in his eyes was human.

"Nuh, nuh, nee—Neanderthal!" said Fig.

"Uh . . . thank you," I said. The creature jumped back in amazement.

"Please, tank you, welcome very much, umsure!" he said.

"You speak English!" I said.

The Neanderthal boy laughed and tapped my lips as though he wanted me to speak again, and when he touched me, I started laughing too.

"What's so funny?" asked Fig.

"I don't know. Him—*he* is. He made me laugh." The creature standing beside the boy growled, and I saw it was an enormous cat with speckled fur and tufted ears.

"It's a lynx!" I said. It looked much larger close up. The Neanderthal put his hand on the cat's neck, and it crouched at his feet, green eyes blazing. The boy helped us up, and we hurried after him as he began to walk toward the ridge.

As we got closer we saw that the cave mouth was half covered with branches. Fig stopped. "I'm not going in there," he said.

"But you said it yourself, we have to. We'll die if we don't!" I remembered something Pa always said: Fear is okay as long as it doesn't stop you. "Fig, I'm scared too."

I took his hand and led him to the entrance, where my own feet seemed to stop all by themselves. The boy looked back, beckoning, and when we didn't move, he seemed puzzled. "Oomor," he said, patting his chest. "Oomor fa-rend, atya service."

"Oomor!" I said. "That must be his name." I touched my own chest, saying, "Allie friend." Then I pointed at my brother. "Fig friend. I'm Allie, he's Fig."

"Ah-lee, Feek. Fa-rend!" said Oomor and walked into the cave.

"We could go in just for a minute, to get warm," I said.

"Yeah, okay, if we stay near the door," said Fig. "Then if there's a cave-in, we can get out."

We stepped inside and waited as Oomor set the torch into a hollow place in the wall and knelt before a ring of stones. He fed dried grass and twigs into a pile of hot embers. As they flamed up he added larger pieces of wood till the fire blazed and we could feel the warmth and see the cave more clearly. Brightly colored paintings of deer, mammoth, horses, bears, and wolves ran along one wall, firewood was stacked against another, and a pile of animal skins made a sort of bed near the hearth. Smoke rose to the ceiling and drifted out the door. It didn't drift out very quickly, though, so the cave was kind of smoky. The lynx came in to lie by the fire and the flames reflected in her eyes. When she yawned, I saw how long and sharp her teeth were. Oomor used a stick to nudge some blackened bundles away from the fire, and when he opened one, it smelled delicious. We drew closer as he scraped the hot food onto flat pieces of bark and handed one to each of us, taking another for himself. Fig and I sat as far away from the cat as possible and tasted the steaming mixture. It was starchy, sweet, and oniony, and we ate it all and licked our fingers.

"That's the best thing I ever ate!" said Fig. Oomor said, "Feek Ah-lee good grub you bet." He stroked the lynx, who began to purr like a hundred Pies. Fig stared at the purring cat and pulled out his notebook and pen.

Something fluttered down from the ceiling and I ducked, thinking it was a bat, but it was only a small brown bird that circled the cave once and landed on Oomor's head. When he reached up, it stepped onto his hand. "Kero," he said. He held it out and the bird hopped onto my finger, tame as anything.

"It's a skylark, I think," said Fig. "I never saw a real one before." He stroked the bird's soft throat with one finger. After a minute the bird darted up to a ledge in the wall and began singing as Oomor picked up a flute carved out of bone. It sounded like the band from Ecuador that plays on our corner in New York, sweet and sad and somehow far away. Fig and I yawned and sank down by the fire, huddled under the furry skins. My eyelids drooped, and the music filled the cave like fog till I fell asleep.

FIG'S NOTEBOOK

DECEMBER 23

I wonder who did the wall paintings. Maybe there are
Cro-Magnon people here too. Cro-Magnons look pretty
much like modern humans, and they did the art in
that cave we went to in Spain when we were eight. Pa
says Neanderthals probably didn't make art. This
Oomor guy walks around with nothing on his feet and
there's snow on the ground! Maybe he'll take us
hunting. He has a blade made of stone and it looks
pretty sharp. Does he have a spear or a bow and
arrows?

I didn't know wild cats could purr. I thought they
were too fierce.

This cave is about 20 feet by 15 feet. If I hadn't
talked her into it, Al probably wouldn't have come in
here and then she'd have frozen to death. I wonder if
Oomor knows how to make fire or if he just has to
find it like those guys in Quest for Fire. I wish I had
my magnifying glass—I'd show him how to make a fire
with the sun.

We must be at least 35,000 years in the past,
maybe a lot more. My watch is gone. I think I left it
in 1913.

CHAPTER EIGHT

I WOKE UP TO THE SOUND OF BIRDS CALLING, AND FOR A minute I thought all our adventures had been a dream and that I was home in my own bed at Yellow House. I opened my eyes to see the cave of my nightmares and jumped up ready to run just as Oomor stepped through the entrance with his arms full of firewood. He set it down, and my heart stopped pounding. I shook Fig to wake him.

We followed Oomor outside as the sun was rising behind the hills. The smell of damp earth and green things growing reminded me so much of springtime at home that I could almost hear Mim and Bijou reciting the daffodil poem. Every April we climb the hill where someone planted a few bulbs long ago. They spread underground and now a zillion daffodils cover the hillside, like tiny golden trumpets against the sky. I saw Mim and Bijou arm in arm chanting into the wind,

"I wandered lonely as a cloud
That floats on high o'er vales and hills,
When all at once I saw a crowd,
A host of golden daffodils."

"Are you crying?" asked Fig.

"The air's cold; it makes my nose run," I said, hunting for a Kleenex. "We're lucky Mary Jobe gave us these clothes yesterday."

"It wasn't yesterday, it was thousands of years in the future," said Fig.

That was too scary and confusing to think about, so I ran to catch up with Oomor. He led us over the ridge onto a high meadow where the sun shone down strong and warm, even early in the morning. Tall grass grew all around, and we could hear birds everywhere. Kero flew overhead, coming down every so often to land on Oomor's shoulder before swooping off after a fly or a grasshopper. I was just wishing I could get some breakfast too, when a herd of horses came galloping over the meadow. They were small with shaggy hides the color of coffee ice cream, and they stopped a short distance away, watching us and flicking their ears. As they lowered their heads to graze, Oomor whistled and walked toward them. He touched a mare on the neck, blowing softly into her nostrils, and she nudged him with her muzzle as he led her away from the others. Her baby trotted close behind.

"Oh, how sweet!" I said, reaching out to the little colt. Its mother shied away at the sound of my voice, and Oomor scowled at me, so I shut up and stood perfectly still. Oomor calmed the mare and squatted beside her, pulling a leather bag from his tunic and holding it in one hand while he milked with the other. Though she kept an eye on Fig and me, she didn't seem to mind.

When the bag was full, Oomor patted the mare, gave her a dried apple, and led us to the edge of the meadow. Oomor handed me the bag and I looked inside. There were hairs floating in the milk, it was warm, and it smelled, well . . . horsey, but I was so hungry I didn't care.

"It's good!" I said and drank several swallows before I remembered the others and gave the bag back to Oomor. He passed it to Fig before he would take his own share, and we sat under the tree drinking milk, eating dried apples and some wrinkled nuts I didn't recognize, and watching the horses.

I wondered how Oomor knew English and why he hardly ever spoke. He *could* speak, obviously. He had names for things and there was nothing wrong with the way he imitated our words, though he had some trouble pronouncing them. So why didn't he speak? I didn't realize I had stopped eating to think, and when I looked up, he was staring at me.

"Ah-lee," he said. "Ah-lee, Feek, Oomor." He touched his mouth and then mine, looking into my eyes so intensely I got dizzy. For a second I felt as though we were one person. Could he be speaking to us with his mind? I decided to see if I could do it too. I thought about Pie but she got all mixed up with other things like Bijou's face, the smell of toast, the feel of carpet under my feet, the sound of the *Lieutenant Kije* Suite from the CD player. I tried to concentrate harder.

Oomor laughed and Fig said, "Why are you making that weird face?"

"I'm trying to talk to him," I said. "He speaks in pictures, in our minds."

"Telepathy! No way!" said Fig.

"Way," I said. "How else could he know English? I'll bet he got it from our minds. Are you sure that's the right word?"

Oomor was muttering and touching his mouth with his fingers as though he were trying to copy us. "Feek, Feek, Feek," he said. "Ah-lee, Ah-lee, Ahhhh . . ." As he spoke I saw pictures rising in my head of Oomor, real and solid, with us looking like smoke, all thin and wispy.

"I see it too!" said Fig. "It *is* telepathy, but he thinks we're ghosts! Or something in a dream; he doesn't know we're real!"

"But we just ate, and you belched," I said. "How could ghosts do that?" Oomor touched my mouth again, and I knew he wanted words, words, and more words.

I took his hand and put my own against it, saying, "Hand. Hand."

"Haaaaah," said Oomor. "Hahnd, hahnd." He pressed his leathery palm against mine and took Fig's hand too. "Hahnd, hahnd, hahnd!" he said and Fig joined in, "Hand! Hand!" We sat for a long time holding hands and chanting the word that suddenly seemed like the most amazing thing in the world, "HAND, HAND, HAND!"

As the days went by we taught him words for all sorts of things and he learned so fast it felt like he was pulling thoughts right out of our brains. He had some trouble with sounds like *dr* and *th,* and kept saying, "dink" for drink and "tie," slapping his leg, "Tie! Tie!"

I put my tongue between my teeth to show him how. "Thhhhigh," I said, "thhhhigh!" When Oomor copied me, he made a sound like a loud fart and he burst out laughing. He did it again, which sent us into a total laughing fit, and every time we started to sober up, someone made the fart sound and set us off again.

At the same time he filled our minds with pictures. They weren't like movies or TV or even those virtual reality things Fig's always talking about. They included smell, touch, taste, sound, and feelings too—so real it was almost too much. No matter how hard we tried we couldn't send pictures back, though I'm sure I passed the idea of words to him somehow. The trouble was, I didn't know how I did it.

"I'll bet it's just him," said Fig. "He's a telepath; that's what people like him are called. If we could do it, we'd have done it before."

"But we do sometimes, like in first grade, when I hit my head on the jungle gym and you were in music with Ms. Transue? You fell off the chair and started crying because your head hurt. That was telepathy for sure."

"Hmmm . . . maybe, but doing it on purpose is different."

That is definitely true. One problem was we could share only the words for things Oomor could understand, like hands, eyes, feet, cold, hot, drink, eat, laugh, run, sleep, fire, bird. How could we make him understand "home" or "time" or "Mim" with nothing but gestures?

"We have to tell him where we came from," I said. "Maybe he can help us."

"How can he? Maybe he can do telepathy, but he can't send us through time," said Fig.

"Fig, we have to get back, we don't fit here. Even if there's only a small chance, we have to try." We were sitting in the cave one evening watching Oomor build the fire. It wasn't just that we were homesick. It was more that we didn't belong here, as though we were wrong pieces forced into a jigsaw puzzle.

"We did try; it just made us go farther back," Fig said. "We need to figure out how it works."

"But we can't stay here—you know we can't."

I noticed Oomor watching us. The firelight was on his face, which didn't seem ugly at all now that I was used to it. I tried to send him a mind-picture. I closed my eyes and imagined the diorama with the Hall of European Mammals around it, and I thought about leaping through the glass into that other time. Nothing happened. Fig still sat poking the fire with a stick; Oomor still crouched, staring into my face. I saw it in my mind, the day we left; I could smell the heat coming up through the old radiators and see how sad Pa's eyes looked as he walked out the door. I saw Mim in her bed, so small and still, and the hurt in Bijou's face that last day. I wrapped both arms around myself to keep from crying.

Suddenly Oomor cried out. He jumped over the fire to land beside me and grab my hand. He was shaking and squeezing my hands, saying all the words we taught him as though he thought it would help. "Hand, dink, water, fie-er, run, hot, hot, Feek, Aahleeahleeah!"

Fig jumped up. "I saw it! You put Mim in my head! I saw her and Bijou. Oh, I want to go home!" All three of us were crying and holding on to each other, and the space behind my eyes ached and throbbed. At last we all calmed down and sat around the hearth sniffling, feeling that empty feeling you get after crying hard. We ate supper without talking, staring into the fire.

Mee Low came in and curled up beside Oomor while I tried to figure out how I had sent the mind-pictures. Oomor kept sending pictures into my head and into Fig's too till we began to see. You have to be calm and still and not try too hard so the pictures can form gradually, like Polaroids. Mine weren't nearly as clear as Oomor's, but each one was better than the last. When Fig tried, he couldn't do it at all, and he scrunched his face up so gruesomely we had to laugh.

Little by little I told our story. Fig could receive pictures even though he couldn't send them, so we hardly spoke. When I thought of Mim, I said her name, and Oomor reached out as though he wanted to touch the face I'd put into his mind. "Flower," he said. "Meem! Mutta Meem." And her smell of lavender, baby powder, and sunblock seemed to fill the cave. I closed my eyes and saw Oomor walking through the forest, leading us toward a doorway that hung in the air with the Hall of European Mammals on the other side. It looked as though we could step right through it into our own time. and I thought it meant Oomor would help us get home. In his vision we were still thin and wispy, like ghosts, or dreams.

"We're as real as you are—realler, even," said Fig, grabbing Oomor's arm and shaking it. He dropped it when the lynx jumped up, growling and lashing her stubby tail. "Mee Low, Mee Low," said Oomor, and he stroked the huge cat till she lay back and began to purr. The sleepy sound made us yawn, and soon we fell asleep, curled up by the fire.

FIG'S NOTEBOOK

DECEMBER 24

Oomor can do telepathy. Allie is learning to do it, but
I can't. I can see it, though, and I don't like it. Pa says
Neanderthals had bigger brains than us. Is that why
Oomor can do it? I wonder if all Neanderthals can do
it, or is it just him? Maybe that's why he doesn't talk
very well. For him telepathy is better. Like for some
deaf people sign language is better than talking. I wish
I could keep him and Allie out of my head. I don't
want to think about Mim all the time, or Bijou or Pa either.

I wish we could've gone skating with Beej.

CHAPTER NINE

EVERY DAY I'D TELL OOMOR MORE ABOUT OUR world. The first time I sent a mind-picture of New York, he choked and covered his head with both arms, so I stopped.

"I think it smells really gross to him," said Fig. "He hates the noise and the too-many people and the stinky air. The air here is . . . new."

I think he's right. There's nothing here but trees and grass, clean rivers and the sound of birds singing, wind in the leaves, fire crackling, water running. Some of the sounds are scary, especially at night, and the thunder seems much louder here than in 2003.

I sat beside Oomor, patting him on the shoulder to calm him down.

"I'll tell him about Yellow House instead of New York, it's more—"

Oomor leapt up. "Nyooyawk!" he said, "Nyooyawk! Kick-lee! Neekalodeen, chollychappin, gettya reddots!"

"Fig, listen! That's not from our heads, he's speaking English. He *knows* English!" I said.

"English? I don't think so, Al, how could he? He's just making sounds, they don't mean anything except for New York, and *you* said that."

"He said, 'Charlie Chaplin' and 'get your red hots'—didn't you hear him? Red hots is what they called hot dogs in the olden days."

"Kicklee!" he said. "Nyooyawk, Kicklee!" The images he was sending were dark and blurry and all I could make out was a tall fat man with a long beard and shaggy hair.

"Hey, I just thought of something. Where are the others?" said Fig suddenly.

"What others?" I asked.

"Where's his family? He's a kid; what's he doing out here all alone?"

I never thought of that. Oomor seems so sure of himself, so at home in his world that I never thought about him having a family. I must have sent him the idea without meaning to because he gasped and jumped up, beckoning for us to follow him out of the cave. We had to move at a fast pace to keep up. His step was so sure and smooth, it was as though he had eyes in his feet. Fig and I had to be careful not to trip over stones or sticks as we hurried after him.

"Maybe he's taking us to his family," I said when Oomor paused for us to catch our breath.

"Maybe." Fig scratched his head and it made my head itch too. I had never been so dirty in my life. It didn't seem to bother my brother.

"Al, I've been thinking about this time thing," he said. "Okay, we're thousands of years ago, we don't know how far. But where are we? Are we still in the Dordogne? And if we are, is Oomor's cave the one where Mim got hurt? We're changing time just by being here. . . . How will that change the future?"

"Maybe it will keep the accident from happening. Maybe we can save Mim!"

"But how do we know what to change? How will we know if it's working?"

I shook my head and walked on, trying to get my mind around the idea of Time. We walked all morning, till we reached the edge of a cliff and a river shining far below.

Oomor said, "Oomor home, Mutta Neema," and pointed down at the valley, hunching up his shoulders as though he were in pain. We saw a settlement beside the river with people going in and out of caves in the cliffs. Some of them paddled round, flat boats near the shore while others gathered around a fire on the bank.

I grabbed Oomor, forgetting to send mind-pictures. "Let's go down there. You can go home, come on!"

He pushed me away so hard I almost fell over the edge, and as he yanked me back I felt a kind of whirlwind in my head, and Fig felt it too. We saw Oomor with Kero on his shoulder, surrounded by his tribe. I recognized the fat, bearded man who handed him the bone flute, the skin bag, and two small stones. Other people came one by one: a woman with flowers in her hair, a man carrying a spear, and several children. When they had all hugged him, they began to sing. It was a strange song, without words, sad and happy at the same time, and they kept on singing as he walked out of the village and into the hills to live alone in his cave.

I pressed my hands against the ache in my head and shut my eyes.

"He's learning to be a sort of priest or magician and Kero is his . . . totem," I said. "He's looking for the place where dreams live, and he thinks that's where we come from, so it's no use trying to explain about home." I looked out over Oomor's valley. His mother and father must have been down there, among the people who sang him away on his journey. I didn't understand why he stayed away if he missed them so much. Home is always on my mind, and on Fig's too, I know. The more time passes, the more it seems like a dream. Mim and Pa and Bijou are as far away as it is possible to be, and the only real things are this hilltop and the cold wind.

"Maybe that's all we are, just his dreams."

"Huh!" said Fig. "Maybe that's all *you* are. I'm real."

When Oomor turned to look at us, I saw two Allies reflected in his eyes.

"Mutta Neema," he said, and I saw the face of the woman in the flower crown.

"His mother—that's his mother," said Fig. The face went blurry like heat haze on a summer street, and then a tornado of light ripped through my brain as blood trickled from my nose. Through the pain I saw Mim's face as though she were right in front of me, and I heard her breathing. I smelled the lavender soap Pa insisted on so she wouldn't smell like the hospital.

"Mutta!" cried Oomor, wiping blood from his own nose, "Mutta Meem, Mutta Neema!"

"Fig, stop! You're too LOUD!" I said.

"I sent a picture! I did it!" Fig shouted, hopping around in a victory dance. He looked so silly I couldn't help laughing even as I pinched my nose to stop the bleeding and rubbed my pounding head. Oomor laughed too, for the first time that day. He took one last look over his valley, and as we walked back down the hill Kero sang overhead.

That night we camped by a brook and watched Oomor start a fire with a handful of dry grass and the two small stones he carried in his skin bag. It took several tries but at last it caught, and he put on twigs and bigger sticks until it blazed up. I never realized how much safer you feel sitting by a fire.

I had a dream that night, and much later Fig told me he had it too. We saw Yellow House with Mim and Pa and Bijou all mixed up with the smell of freshly baked bread and the hum of our old refrigerator. We were all together by the fireplace, telling ghost stories, and then Pa took out his guitar and began to sing old songs.

"Lean on me, when you're not strong, and I'll be your friend. I'll help you carry on . . ."

I wonder if Oomor dreamed about his family too, all sitting around a fire in a big, smoky cave. Fig doesn't think so, but I do. We're more the same than we are different.

Next day we were all more cheerful, and everything seemed hopeful, the way it usually does in the morning. Fig and I talked about breakfast. We were so hungry after yesterday, and I thought about bacon and eggs and pancakes so hard that Oomor laughed and rubbed his belly. "Eat food!" he said. He led us to the brook and pulled out handfuls of smooth black mussels. We picked the biggest ones to roast in the fire, and the smell reminded me of the oyster and clam roasts we have in Maine. Bijou always makes tarragon butter sauce to go with the shellfish. Last year Pa and Mim came for the last weekend before we went back with them to Yellow House, and Pa made garlic mustard butter. He and Bijou always talked about food. Sometimes I wish that Pa had married Bijou instead of Mim. I used to think I'd like to stay in the city all year and take art classes with Beej. I get so bored at Yellow House after a while, especially in winter. Bijou says, "Be careful what you wish for," and she's right. Living in New York City has been horrible; everything is all messed up.

While the mussels were cooking I knelt by the brook and washed my face and hands as well as I could in the icy water, trying not to think about hot showers and shampoo.

Oomor pulled the bark off a dead tree stump and I said, "Oh, gross!" It was swarming with huge white worms. I made myself watch as he speared them onto small twigs and set them to toast on the fire.

I felt better after we ate the mussels, until Oomor picked up a twig full of toasted worms and took a bite. A sour liquid filled the back of my throat, and I looked away. When I looked back, Fig was holding a twig and chewing.

"Fig!" I said. He swallowed and looked surprised.

"They're good!" he said, taking another worm kebab.

"Dee-lishus, eat food, hits the spot!" said Oomor as he held one out to me. I wasn't going to hurt his feelings, and for sure I wasn't going to let my brother be the brave one, so I shut my eyes and bit down. They were crunchy and greasy, sort of like french fries without salt, so I pretended as hard as I could that that's what they were. I drank water and tried not to think about what I had eaten.

"Yum!" I said, patting my belly and hoping I wouldn't throw up.

I didn't, and it was the first time I'd felt almost full since we landed in the Ice Age. We spent most of every day looking for food, and even so we were always hungry. On the way back from the cliff we collected some turtle eggs Oomor found not far from a river bank. Even though there were lots of them, he only took two from each nest. Each egg was hardly a mouthful, and we had to share the fourth one. Oomor doesn't seem to hunt animals or eat meat, even though his tunic is made of fur, and he always uses the word "brother" or "sister" when he talks about animals or birds. I didn't think he understood what "brother" and "sister" mean, but Fig said he did. He thinks it's why Oomor doesn't hunt or eat anything but nuts, fruits, and vegetables.

"And mussels," I said. "Maybe he won't eat things with faces."

"Bugs have faces; faces and gooey, gooshy guts—yum yum!"

My stomach heaved, but I wasn't about to let my brother know it.

"Pa says lots of people eat bugs," I said. "Look at that *Food Insects Newsletter* he gets; it even has recipes."

"Squish! Pop!" said Fig. I turned my back. Sometimes I think boys are a whole different species.

After breakfast we walked on, feeling sleepy with our bellies finally full and the sun getting warmer. The trees were covered with buds, and green shoots that looked like crocuses or snowdrops poked up through the ground. Oomor's cave almost felt like home that evening, and I don't think I'll ever be scared of caves anymore. I haven't had the nightmare about Mim since we came through the diorama, and neither has Fig.

Fig says if I'm telling this story, I should tell the embarrassing parts, not just the exciting and fun stuff. So I will, but I hope nobody sees this till I'm dead.

The thing is, I really hate camping, and this is camping all the time. When Mim and Pa take us on trips, we camp half the time and stay in hotels the other half because Mim likes camping and Pa doesn't. He loves hotels, and so do I. They're so clean, and you don't have to pick up after yourself. They have all these neat little soaps and shampoos, and a TV in the room, and room service. I don't see why Fig couldn't go camping with Mim, then Pa and I could go to a nice hotel. The way we do it, someone is always going to be unhappy.

Hiking is okay but all the other camping stuff is gross, like going to the bathroom in the bushes. You have to cover it up with dirt like Pie does in her litter pan, and peeing is harder for girls than boys. Number two with leaves for toilet paper is just plain disgusting. Even in a fancy campground with toilets, you never know if there are spiders or snakes.

In the Ice Age, I felt dirty all the time. Oomor broke through the skim of ice on the brook every morning to wash himself all over, hollering and splashing. I couldn't stand it, so I just dabbed my face, and Fig didn't even bother. My hair was greasy, and I was really glad I didn't grow it out like Bijou wanted me to. Even so, it got all matted till Oomor showed me how to comb out the knots with my fingers. I was sure I'd get lice, and we already had fleas. A few days after we landed in the Ice Age we were sitting by the fire and Fig was scratching his head. Oomor said, "Dreh, dreh!" and got up to sit facing him. He reached out to Fig with both hands, ducking his head and smiling. Fig pulled back at first, but then he sat still as Oomor began to comb through his hair, strand by strand, every now and then putting his fingers in his mouth. They looked just like the apes in the zoo.

"Omigosh, Fig, he's *eating* your fleas—picking them out and eating them!" My brother's eyes were half closed, and if he'd been a cat, he'd have been purring. It wasn't long before Oomor was grooming my hair too, and I have to admit, it felt pretty good. Fig did it for Oomor, but he didn't eat the fleas; he just cracked them between his fingernails. In a way, Oomor was very clean; he even taught us how to use a twig to brush our teeth. His teeth were white and strong looking so I guess the twig is almost as good as brushing and flossing. Of course there was no candy to rot his teeth. The dried apples and berries were hardly sweet at all, not even as sweet as raisins.

In my own time I'd always wished I'd get my period, like Cissy Baker and Melina Romero, but now I was *so* glad I hadn't! It embarrassed me to even think about it; I don't know what I would have done if I'd gotten it. I had no privacy at all. The first few nights I slept a little way from Oomor and my brother, but it was so cold at night, even with the fire, that we all had to sleep close together under Oomor's furry animal skins. In the morning we were all tangled up, and I had to pull my arms and legs out from under the others'. I don't see how married people can stand to sleep with each other, it is so gross.

Sometimes I thought if we ever got home I would take about ten boiling-hot showers and stay in a really nice hotel like the Carlyle for a month. And then I'd have my own room with a lock on the door and a sign that said, KEEP OUT! THIS MEANS YOU!

FIG'S NOTEBOOK

DECEMBER 25

Today is Christmas. Al doesn't know. If we were at Yellow House, we'd all have gone out last night to look at the sky. You can't see many stars in NYC because there's too much ambient light, but in the country you can see millions without a telescope. Here you can see even more.

I did telepathy today and it hurt. Al says I have to relax to do it right. Oomor is a shaman, which is like a doctor plus a magician only not like those lame guys on TV with card tricks. Anyhow, magic is just a word for things science hasn't figured out yet. If Mim and Beej and Pa were here, I'd really like this, only Beej would hate it without hot baths and French shampoo. She has really pretty hair.

I'm not too good at relaxing.

CHAPTER TEN

ONE NIGHT OOMOR SHOWED US HOW TO PAINT handprints on the wall. He took bits of charcoal from the hearth and chewed them, and then he pressed his hand flat against the wall with the fingers spread out and sprayed the charcoal spit through his lips. When he took his hand away, there was a perfect print on the stone. "Hand!" he said, pointing. Fig and I tried, but the charcoal tasted terrible and made us choke. We couldn't do a fine spray like Oomor; it just came out in slimy gray blobs. We rinsed our mouths and then Oomor did our handprints next to his.

"It's just like the stencils Bijou did at Yellow House!" I said.

"Except for the spit," said Fig.

Oomor took more charcoal, crushed it on the hearthstone, and mixed it with some greasy paste he had wrapped in a leaf.

"It's mashed larvae," said Fig. "I saw him save some from breakfast yesterday."

I thought he was just trying to gross me out, but he was right. We sat watching Oomor draw the animals we'd seen on our long walk. He works fast, like Bijou does. He did horses, mammoths, a saber-toothed cat, hawks, bison, and one of the big deer whose antlers are so wide you'd think it would fall over.

"You can really see what they are," said Fig, who isn't very good in art. We watched Oomor draw a picture of Mee Low standing on her hind legs and stretching to sharpen her claws. Fig is right; Oomor is better than Bijou or Gordon or anyone I ever saw.

"They're beautiful," I said. "He's a real artist."

"Beej would love this, and Mim and Pa. . . . Allie, that's it! This must be the cave! If these pictures are here in our time, it's just where Mim and Pa would go!" Fig jumped up, and Oomor turned to look at him. I pointed to the drawings, sending a question to his mind. He touched them, one by one. "Brother," he said, "sister," and went back to painting, humming a tune through his nose.

"What should we do?"

"To change things?" said Fig. "We already have, just by being here and leaving our handprints and being with Oomor." His face looked grim.

"Only we don't know how we've changed things," I said, speaking in a whisper. Fig nodded and sat down again, chewing on his thumb.

The last thing Oomor drew was himself in black and Fig and me in white, yellow, and red paint he got from containers made out of mussel shells. He worked more carefully with the colors, as though they were scarce and precious, and then he drew a black square around Fig and me, with us waving as though we were saying goodbye. Finally, he reached up as high as he could and drew a woman with big hips and bosoms and a round belly. Her hair was braided into a crown on her head and you couldn't tell if she was young or old, but her face was calm and wise. I feel like I've seen her somewhere before.

"Fig," I said, "let's draw something, here on the wall, something from our own time. That will change things for sure." My brother stood up and stared at the wall.

"Yeah, it would, I think. You know what could happen?" I knew. Terrible things. Us changing just one small thing in this time could start a . . . chain of events, I think it's called, so the future, *our* future could be nuclear war or a man-made plague or pollution killing everything. Or it might be that we're never born at all. I shivered. "I know," I said.

"I can't draw," said Fig.

"It doesn't have to be art," I said, picking up a mussel shell full of black paint. Oomor smiled at me and stood back to watch. I found a bare spot on the wall near the torch and began to paint with my thumb. I added red and a little yellow mixed together, and some spots of white for the windows. Oomor made an admiring hiss through his teeth.

"That's good," said Fig. "It's the museum. The tower looks really real." I stepped back and handed him the black paint. He stood staring at the wall for a minute and then dipped his pointer finger into the paint and wrote on the wall: $E=mc^2$.

"There," he said. Einstein's equation. I don't understand

what it means, and I don't think Fig does either, but I know it changed the world. I almost expected something to happen, the sound of the universe cracking, maybe, but nothing did.

Oomor was really happy and excited about our paintings. He pointed to mine and looked at me.

"American Museum of Natural History in New York City, in the year 2003," I said.

"Ahhh!" said Oomor. He pointed to Fig's formula—Einstein's I mean.

"E=mc²," said Fig. "The theory of relativity: energy equals matter times the speed of light, squared."

"Ahhh!" said Oomor again, and he pointed to the woman he had drawn on the wall.

"Ah Bah Mutta," he said, and I was surprised to see tears running down his face even though he was smiling.

"Feek, Ah-lee, home, Nyooyawk," he said.

"Maybe that picture is magic," I said. "He thinks it'll help us go home."

"No such thing as magic. Anyhow, how could it?" said Fig. "It's just a painting." Then his face lit up. "But so was the diorama; just a painting and some stuffed animals!"

I grabbed his hand. "Listen, Fig, the other two times we spun to the right didn't we? Maybe if we spin to the left, we'll go forward instead of back!"

Fig's face turned pink with excitement as he pulled me to my feet. Oomor came up to us and put the bone flute in Fig's hand and the bag holding the firestones in mine. I knew he would die without fire so I shook my head, but he insisted.

"We should give him something too," I said. Fig rummaged in his pockets and pulled out a dried apple core, a Popsicle stick, two jelly beans covered with lint, a rubber spider, a heart-shaped stone, some string, a piece of chalk, and a ticket stub from *Beyond Jurassic Park*. He gave Oomor the spider and the chalk. I felt around in my pockets. There wasn't anything but a LifeSaver and a string of beads Pa had brought me from Africa. Then my hand touched the dreidel and I remembered something from one of Pa's stories: "The most precious gift is the hardest to give." The dreidel felt comforting and familiar in my hand, and I could hear Mim singing the song that went with it. It was all I had of her. I tucked it deeper in my pocket and put the beads around Oomor's neck. "Brother, Sister, Feek, Ah-lee," he said, and he hugged us. As he stepped back he began chanting the same song his people sang when he went away.

We began spinning to the left, going faster and faster, till the cave seemed to blur and dissolve into gray mist just like before. Then suddenly the mist turned to boiling-hot steam and smoke as flame and burning lava whirled and roared around us. My lungs were on fire, and when I reached out to Fig, I heard him screaming!

All at once something grabbed us and yanked us out of the fire into wonderfully cool fresh air, and when I opened my eyes, we were back in the cave with Oomor holding us by the wrists, crying, "Ah-lee, Feek! Feek, Ah-lee, ah!"

We sat up slowly, moving our arms and legs to make sure nothing was burned or broken. Except for sore throats and teary eyes we were okay, but our clothes had turned brown and brittle like dead leaves in autumn, and our faces and arms were bright red, as though we'd been sunburned. Oomor held a gourd full of water to Fig's lips. He grabbed it, gulped half of it down, and and handed the gourd to me.

"We went into the past again," he said hoarsely. "Way back to when Earth was forming, before there was land or sea or anything. We can only go back and back. We'll never get home."

"Oomor saved us; he saved our lives," I said.

"I know. I know he did." He put his face down on his knees. I couldn't talk anymore. I had almost killed us and talking wouldn't help. I wondered what it would be like to grow up with Neanderthals, and whether Bijou and Pa would care that we were gone. Would Mim ever wake up, and if she did, would she even remember us?

Oomor crouched near, patting us and saying our names over and over. He began to sing.

"Dis ole man he play wan, he play niknok oh my tum—"

"It was you!" said Fig, raising his head. "You were following us."

We joined in, singing in croaky voices like crows.

"Knick-knack paddywhack, give a dog a bone. This old man came rolling home."

Sometimes singing is better than talking.

FIG'S NOTEBOOK

JANUARY 15

We've really done it now. We drew on the wall and
changed the future for sure. Then Allie's idea nearly
killed us. Maybe we can't go forward. I keep thinking
of my watch somewhere in 1913 where it doesn't
belong. What's that going to change?

None of this would've happened if Mim and Pa
didn't go away every year. Sometimes I think they don't
even want to be parents, but then at Yellow House
they are pretty cool. Mim chases me around trying to
hug me and not catching me on purpose. Pa and I play
chess for hours. I always hate it when they leave us
with Beej in June. Beej says, "One day for a pity
party," and I go to my room and play computer games
and read and don't talk to anyone. After that I'm okay.
She's a really great aunt.

Oomor saved our lives.

CHAPTER ELEVEN

T HE NEXT DAY, AS WE GATHERED FOOD FOR THE evening, Fig and I talked about why my idea didn't work. We weren't much good at food gathering because we didn't know which plants are good to eat, so Oomor had us catching snails to roast in the fire. I'd eaten snails with garlic butter in French restaurants so I was pretty sure a snail wasn't a bug. A restaurant wouldn't serve bugs, at least not on purpose. Snails must be some kind of shellfish, I thought, finding a big one and dropping it into the windbreaker we were using for a bag.

Fig keeps saying my idea didn't just not work, it almost killed us. It is really annoying when someone keeps telling you something you already know. Even if it didn't work, it *was* brilliant, or at least logical. Fig always says I'm not logical, but my idea was. He had to admit it seemed like a good idea, but neither of us can figure out why it failed.

"Don't say I almost killed us again; I can't stand it!" I said.

"Well, how can we get home then?"

We sat under an oak tree and went over our three trips in time again and again. Why had we whirled so easily into the Ice Age, and why couldn't we go back to our own time?

"Or forward," said Fig. We thought for a while. We were pretty sure Mary Jobe brought us to the right place, so why didn't it work? Why didn't we spin right back into the Hall of European Mammals?

"Allie, maybe it's just not possible to go forward. I mean, the past has already happened, so it's real, but the future hasn't, it's not set."

"But it is, sort of. We remember it, we've been there, we're *from* there." It was so complicated, like a knot we couldn't untie. We sat thinking for a long time under the tree with the bag full of snails clicking softly beside us. Suddenly Fig jumped up shouting, "I know! I know!" so loud that Oomor came running.

"I bet the lynxes weren't there anymore," he said, talking so fast he tripped over the words. "Don't you get it, Mary Jobe stopped André from shooting them so they weren't ever in the museum. We changed the past so things were different in our own time. We couldn't go back through the lynx diorama because *it wasn't there!*" It was so confusing it made me dizzy, and the more Fig explained, the more confused I got.

"Go on, tell it to him," said Fig.

"How can I? I don't understand it myself!"

We all sat down with our backs against the tree to figure things out. I watched Oomor as he picked up an acorn and spun it like a top on a flat stone. It kept falling over. I reached into my pocket. "I have a better top than that," I said, setting the point of the dreidel on the stone and giving it a twirl.

A light flashed through my brain, surrounding Oomor with twinkling spots of color like the lights you see behind your eyelids when you squeeze your eyes tight shut. He pointed at the dreidel and sent us a mind-picture more complete than any we had seen before. We saw him as a baby sleeping in a nest of fur, and as we watched, the dreidel appeared over his head. As he woke up and reached out, it vanished, and he began to cry. We saw him again as a toddler, sitting with the shaman as the dreidel appeared again. Finally we saw Oomor the age he is now, with garlands of lilies and rosemary around his neck, holding the dreidel and dancing through a doorway into a place full of music and light, rainbow-striped and shining, with Fig and me behind him. The picture disappeared and left us gasping for breath, as though we had stayed under water too long.

"He's seen the dreidel in his dreams," said Fig slowly, "ever since he was a baby. It's why they chose him to be the next shaman. He went on his journey to find it. It's his, his . . ."

"Grail," I said, "like the Holy Grail. He's been on a quest."

"Yeah, that's it," said Fig.

"So maybe the dreidel is the key to getting back. If we only knew how to use it. . . ." I said. I made myself calm down and sent Oomor a picture of us going through the doorway holding the dreidel. He laughed and shook his head, pointing at himself and then at me.

"Brother, sister," he said. Then he curled his hands into

claws and snarled like a cat. "Mee Low, brother," he said. He touched the dreidel. "No brother, no sister." Did he mean that only a living creature can travel through time? Maybe that's the key.

"Oh, Fig, I don't think it's the dreidel. It's Oomor himself. He's the boy in the case—he's Dreidel Boy!"

"You don't know that. It's only a skeleton; it could be anybody."

"What about the big bead in his hand; that's the dreidel, Fig. I'm sure it is. I just know it's him. He thinks we're part of his quest and he wants to take us home. And if he does, he'll die."

Fig sat thinking, chewing on his thumb.

"Then tell him no, send a picture. We'll figure out another way."

I did tell him, with words and mind-pictures, but I could see that Oomor didn't get it. His face was all pink with happiness as he called Kero, who flew down from his perch and began to sing.

No matter how hard I tried I couldn't make Oomor understand why we didn't want him to go. He showed us the magic doorway again and again, and after a while we began to see that for him, death isn't like it is for us. Fig and I have never even seen a dead person except on television, but Oomor saw his baby sister die the day she was born. His uncle was killed by a poisonous snake, his best friend was crushed to death in a rock slide, and his mother's mother died of cold the previous winter. Death was normal to him, and the spirit world was as real to him as Disneyland is for us. Even if you've never been to Disneyland, you know it's there. Oomor's people think it's a great honor to follow a dream to the other side of death.

Oomor curled up by the fire and went to sleep, and Fig and I stayed up, talking in whispers. It was no use. We were sure that if we went back to our own time with Oomor, he would die.

"He can't make us go," I said.

"We'll go without him," said Fig.

"How?"

"I don't know how. I don't *know!*" Fig stood up and stomped to the cave entrance. I went to stand beside him, and we looked out over the Ice Age world, all silvery in the moonlight.

"It's beautiful here," I said at last.

"We'll never have to go to school, or to the dentist," said Fig. A flock of birds flew across the moon, calling to each other in the night. Mim's face and Pa's and Bijou's filled my mind.

"I wish we hadn't been so mean to Bijou," said Fig. I took my brother's hand.

"What's black and white and black and white and green?" Fig took a deep breath and rubbed his eyes hard.

"Two penguins eating a pickle," he said. We turned back toward the fire and lay down beside our friend.

FIG'S NOTEBOOK

JANUARY 16

I still don't get why Allie's idea didn't work. I wish I could go online or to the library to find out. I don't know if Al is right that Oomor will die if he helps us get home, but I know we can't take the chance. Oomor is our friend. We'll have to figure out how to get home behind his back.

But if we're going to stay here, I'm going to invent some things, like pottery. There's clay by the brook, and we took a class with Beej two years ago. Also medicine like aspirin from willow bark and penicillin from bread mold. We don't have any bread, but I bet I can invent that too.

When I think of Bijou, I see her face when I said she wasn't our mother. Only little kids believe you can take words back once you've said them. You can't.

CHAPTER TWELVE

OOMOR WAS THE STUBBORNEST PERSON I'D EVER known. No matter how often I told him Fig and I were going to stay, he'd just ignore me and sing to himself or wrap new treasures in a piece of deerskin. He told us he didn't know the magic to send us home, so we all set out to ask the shaman for help. Oomor gave us each a handful of acorns, took the skin bag to fill at the brook, and tucked his knife into the strip of hide at his waist.

"You have to make him see, Al. We need time to figure out how to get home by ourselves."

"I'm trying!" My head ached with sending thoughts. "Why don't *you* do it, you're way louder than I am."

"I don't know how I did it that time; it just came. You have to try harder, Allie."

"Just shut up, okay? Just leave me alone." Oomor walked in just then, and I closed my mouth like a trap.

The sun was rising as he led us outside with Kero perched

on his head, leaving Mee Low asleep in the cave. The sky was so pretty it reminded me of Mim at Yellow House. Dawn is my mother's favorite time of day and mine too. No matter how early I wake up at home, Mim is up before me, curled in an armchair by the window with one of the neighbor's cats on her lap and a cup of tea beside her. Sometimes I watch her for a long time before she sees me standing there. Then she puts down the cat and I climb into her lap for a cuddle.

The last time she said, "Look at all those knobby knees!" We were kind of squashed in with our legs tangled up. "You're getting too big for this, Allie Bally Bee."

"Not too big for cuddling," I said, smelling her morning smell of sleep, baby powder, and jasmine tea.

Mim brushed my hair back and put her nose right up to mine so we both went cross-eyed. "Nope," she said. "Never too big for that, no way, no how."

When I looked up, Fig was scowling, and I wondered if he had seen my thoughts.

"I hate it when you put Mim in my head; I don't want to think about her."

"I can't help it; I miss her too, Fig. I'm sorry," I reached for his hand but he pulled away. Oomor turned and watched us as we hurried to catch up.

There wasn't any wind, and as the sun rose higher, it got very warm. We had to work hard to keep up with Oomor, which kept us slightly out of breath. He was so interested in learning more words, and he was in such a good mood that we caught it, like a cold.

There were millions of dandelions growing all over the

meadow, so Fig picked one and said, "Dan-dee-lie-on." It was a hard word for Oomor; its syllables wound around his tongue. "Daddeladda!" he said, and "Dan-da-dadlin! Diddle-de-dan!"

When the sun was high, we stopped to eat. We were munching acorns and clover shoots when Kero flew into the air twittering frantically. Suddenly the earth heaved, throwing us flat and tearing the meadow into jagged chunks with a terrible roaring, like a beast in pain. At last it stopped, and we sat up and looked around. Oomor dragged us behind a fallen tree just as a herd of enormous deer stampeded across the meadow. The ground shook under their hooves. When the earth was still, Kero swooped down onto Oomor's shoulder and began to preen his ruffled feathers. We picked up our things and stumbled on. Now Oomor hurried us along over the torn earth, and when I tripped and fell, he just pulled me up and said, "Satoro, oora ama. Satoro!"

We had to jump over deep cracks and climb around hunks of dirt thrown up by the earthquake, and when we finally reached the top of the hill, we found our path had been chopped off as neatly as if a giant had sliced it with a knife. Instead of a trail leading into Oomor's valley there was only a sheer cliff with no way down. Now and then an aftershock sent a landslide of rocks and dirt crashing into the ravine and brought a thick cloud of dust boiling up from the valley. You couldn't see the village or the river or anything but brown dust.

We backed away from the dangerous edge, and since the sun was low in the sky, we decided to camp at the foot of the hill.

We could see that Oomor was worried without reading

mind-pictures. He didn't know if his people had survived, and he didn't know how to get down to see if they had. He took the firestones from me without a word and built a fire. We spent the night huddled around it, listening, wondering, and waiting for dawn.

FIG'S NOTEBOOK

JANUARY 17

I think the earthquake happened because I wrote
$E=mc^2$. Or maybe it's my watch back in 1913, like a
bomb waiting to go off. Al is right, we don't belong
here; we don't fit.

If I ever get home, I'm going to be a mathematician
or an astrophysicist. I'll bet scientists like Einstein
and Stephen Hawking never worry about anything.
Stephen Hawking has amyotrophic lateral sclerosis.
I've seen him. He's paralyzed, in a wheelchair, and he
talks through a computer.
I wonder if he's so used to it that now he's like
it says in *The Mysterious Stranger*, "a thought . . .
and indestructible." Just this huge, great mind; a
brain that can't be hurt.

Beej gave me my watch for my ninth birthday. I
wish I hadn't lost it.

CHAPTER THIRTEEN

IN THE MORNING THE SKY WAS HAZY WITH DUST AND there was a green ring around the sun. We had no breakfast, and when I tried to speak to Oomor, he didn't seem to hear. He said "Come" and began to walk east along the foot of the hill so quickly we had to jog to keep up. The more I try not to think about food the more I think about Bijou's breakfasts. I don't mean regular breakfasts, where everybody eats sensible things like toast and cereal and then goes off to school and work. I mean special mornings like stormy Saturdays, or birthdays, or first day of summer vacation. Bijou makes weird yummy things like kedgeree or chicken livers on toast or chilequiles, and we sit around eating and planning the day. She's a way better cook than Mim; we always put on weight in the summer. Once I said to Fig that if you could put Mim and Beej into a blender, you'd get the perfect mother, but he got really mad. He thinks Mim is perfect. He says Bijou is okay but "too emotional,"

whatever that means. He likes her cooking though. And she always has neat ideas for stuff to do, like looking for the enchanted cottage on Charles Street, or going to Pearl Paints or the fortune cookie factory on Pell Street. Tourists don't know about those things, only people who've lived in New York all their lives do, like Beej. I was thinking about her stirring a pot of mushroom risotto and singing "The Logger's Lament," when I tripped over a root.

When I fell down for the third time, I got mad and wouldn't let Fig help me up. He made a face and walked ahead, slashing at the ground with a stick. Gradually the path rose into a meadow covered with grass and patches of blackberry bramble. The ground was smoother and a breeze had blown away the dust. The air smelled of green things growing, and the sun was warm on my face. I was really starving by this time so I ran to catch up with Oomor, but when I sent him thoughts of food, he shook his head and walked on.

Around noon we stopped to rest. Oomor gathered insects—ants, earthworms, and beetle larvae—and crushed them in his palm until he had a handful of lumpy brown paste. He held out his hand. "Good grub eat," he said. I turned away just in time to keep from throwing up on his arm. Fig looked at the bug paste while I retched into the grass. He handed me this tiny shred of Kleenex from his pocket and rubbed my back like Mim does when we're sick. The scrap of Kleenex was so small and dirty and pathetic it made me laugh, and then I choked.

"You okay, Al?" I wiped my mouth, took a drink from the water bag, and nodded.

"Eat!" said Oomor.

"Thanks, Oomor," said Fig. "We're not very hungry." Oomor shrugged and ate the bugs, licking his palm till it was clean. There was only enough water left for two swallows each, and there were no streams in sight. We had no idea how long it would take to get to the valley, and Oomor couldn't tell us, either because he didn't know or because he doesn't think of time and distance as people do in 2003. There was no choice but to keep walking.

I was beginning to think the endless green flatness would go on forever when suddenly the wind changed, and I smelled something familiar. I looked around to see a herd of mammoth moving slowly over the plain, grazing on the thick grass. Oomor hooted and raced toward them, leaving us behind, and the lead mammoth hooted back. She waited with the herd behind her while Fig and I followed Oomor, walking more and more slowly as the mammoths loomed up before us. Up close they weren't like elephants at all, in spite of the smell; no more than a wolf is like a chihuahua. Fig's fists were clenched, and I could hear my heart pounding as Oomor walked right up to the creatures that looked like monsters out of a nightmare: dark, shaggy, and terrible. The leader reached out and touched his face with her trunk while the others swayed their huge bodies as though they were dancing to welcome him. I knew they wouldn't hurt us as long as we were with him.

The mammoths towered over us like hairy mountains, and I shut my eyes as the leader explored my head with the tip of her trunk. I opened them when I heard Oomor laughing. He patted my arm with one hand and the mammoth's trunk with the other. "Sister, sister," he said, still laughing.

That afternoon was like a dream circus. The lead mammoth knelt while Oomor helped us climb onto her neck. Then he scrambled up himself and we went riding across the plain, high above the grass. They took us to a grove of birch trees where a tiny spring bubbled out of the ground, and we drank and filled the skin bag. When we looked up, the two biggest mammoths were tearing strips of bark off the trees, and Oomor showed us how to peel and eat the inside part, which smelled kind of like wintergreen LifeSavers. It wasn't very filling, but it was better than nothing. We climbed aboard again and rode on, swishing through the tall grass, and it was so warm and comfortable snuggled between Oomor and the mammoth's big ears that Fig and I fell asleep.

FIG'S NOTEBOOK

JANUARY 18

I can feel my ribs and see Allie's backbone under her sweatshirt when she bends over. I read that if you don't eat anything, after a while you don't feel hungry anymore, but here we eat something almost every day, only it's never enough. At first I thought about cheeseburgers and fries all the time, but now I think about Bijou's Japanese soup. It's clear and there's watercress and thin slices of mushroom and chicken in it and rice at the bottom. She made it for me last June, when I had a cold. She brought it on a tray with her homemade crackers for me to eat in bed. "Summer colds are the *worst*, Figlet," she said, and she read to me from *Scientific American*.

CHAPTER FOURTEEN

W E WOKE TO SEE A MOB OF NEANDERTHALS running toward us yelling and waving sticks and clubs. The mammoths halted and the four babies ran into the center of the herd for protection. Oomor leapt down to stand in front of them with his arms spread. The people shouted his name and one man stepped forward, glaring at Oomor and shaking a long spear. When he saw Fig and me peeking out from behind our mammoth's ears, he jumped back. "Ahhbbaaa!" he said. "Ah Bah!"*

Oomor took his arm, saying, "Tem! Ah-lee, Feek, Ah Bah Neh Kicklee. Satoro beh?"

"Beh, wenda," said Tem, never taking his eyes off us. We climbed down to face the Neanderthals, and my head filled

*translation: "Spirits! spirts of the Dreamtime!
"Tem! Allie, Fig, *Good* spirits like Kicklee. What news of the earthquake?"
"All is well."

with confused pictures of us all thin and stretched out with glowing blue eyes and flaming hair. I heard loud crackling like static that must have come from too many mind-pictures at once. "Tem. Ah-lee, Feek, Ah Bah Neh!" said Oomor. Tem shook his spear, sending an image of a mammoth lying dead, bleeding from a dozen wounds, and the mammoth leader must have seen it too because she reared up with a scream, sending the Neanderthals falling all over themselves in terror. She turned and led the herd away, trotting heavily across the plain as the people shouted and shook their weapons. Some of the Neanderthals chased after them a little way but then turned back, muttering. As the mammoths vanished over the horizon the tribe approached us, staring and whispering, and Fig and I edged behind Oomor. He took our hands and led us back the way the hunters had come. The others followed behind. My head filled with static again, and I couldn't understand anything.

"They're talking about the earthquake," said Fig, "and something about the mammoths and a feast, I think."

We stopped to rest, and the hunters offered us roasted eggs and a sort of doughcake made of pounded acorns and honey. The three youngest hunters came closer, giggling and shoving each other. They seemed fascinated by our clothes, but when I took off one of my red Reeboks, they backed away screaming, "Ah Bah! Ah Bah!"

Oomor came running, saying, "Ah Bah Neh Kicklee."

Fig said, "They think you're taking off your feet!" That made me laugh, and the hunters laughed too when I showed them how the Reeboks came on and off. The oldest girl tried to put one on, but it was much too small. They all sniffed them and put them on their hands, and everybody watched me put them back on and lace them up. I think they could have watched me take my shoes off and put them on all day.

After a while we walked on down a long, winding path to the valley. As we got closer and closer to the village I started to see Mim the way I saw her in my nightmares, crushed under the rocks. I tried to keep the thoughts away but they kept rising in my head like smoke.

"NO!" shouted Fig. "Stop it, Al—please don't!"

"I'm not doing anything. It just comes into my mind and won't go away. Fig, what if Oomor's cave isn't the one? What if it happened here?"

"What if it did? We have no way of knowing. We've changed about a million things accidentally and on purpose, Al. Don't you see, our world might not even be there anymore!" I wished he wouldn't keep reminding me. No Mim, no Bijou, no Pa. I remembered the skull in the museum and thought of Oomor's face like a mask over the bones.

"It doesn't matter anyhow," I said. "We're not going back with him. He can't make us, even if he won't listen." We walked on, with the three hunters giggling and whispering behind us.

By the time we got near the valley the dust had settled, and we could see the village and the people waving and calling from below. Oomor and the hunters shouted for joy and ran helter-skelter down the trail while we followed behind them.

Three women and two old men stood waiting at the bottom, while five little kids came running to meet us, jumping and pushing till the grownups chased them away. No one was killed in the quake, though most of them had bumps, bruises, and cuts from falling rocks. The river was muddy, and all the fires had gone out, but they had already begun cleaning up.

One of the women ran to us and threw her arms around Oomor, rubbing her face against his. When she stepped back, he said, "Neema Mutta. Oomor Mutta." She smiled shyly, reaching out to touch our faces, and she gasped when she saw our eyes were blue, like Oomor's. "Oomor, Ah Bah, Kicklee Ah Bah!" she said, looking from him to us, back and forth, again and again. Her own eyes, like the eyes of all the other Neanderthals, were dark brown, so I guess blue eyes are really unusual for them.

Then, as though there had been a signal, everyone turned toward the caves, chanting, "Kicklee, Kicklee." We watched as a tall, fat, bearded man came out, wearing a pair of glasses with one stem missing.

"Hieronymous Quigley, at your service," he said.

FIG'S NOTEBOOK

JANUARY 19

There has to be a way back. If M&P had let us skip another grade, I'd know more math and science. I could've taken that summer class at Columbia where they do beginning physics and calculus if M hadn't had the accident. I told P I could do it on my own, but he said it would be "too much." I don't get that. Too much for who?

Maybe A and O are wrong and getting home has nothing to do with using a living creature. I'm pretty sure the spinning comes into it somehow.

These Neanderthals have some pretty good tools and weapons. They mostly look just like rocks at first, and then you see how well they fit into your hand and how sharp the edges are. I wish I had my Swiss Army knife.

Quigley. Another artist. We need someone who can think. We need a scientist.

CHAPTER FIFTEEN

"QUIGLEY!" I CRIED.

"You're no ghost," said Fig.

"Far from it, young fella me lad," said Quigley. He wore skins like the Neanderthals, but there was a scrap of cloth sticking out from under his beard that might once have been a red and blue necktie; a shabby pair of boots were on his feet. His bright blue eyes peered closely at my brother and me as he held his glasses on with one hand.

"Late twentieth century, I should think. Am I right?"

"Uh, yes, well, early twenty-first, actually," I said. "What are *you* doing here?"

"Trip through time, same as you I daresay, eh?" We nodded, too surprised to speak.

"Well, come along, come along. A bite to eat would not be unwelcome, from the look of you. Grub's not half bad, though it's no Delmonico's. What I wouldn't give for a lobster

Newburg or a bottle of the aught-six." He put an arm around Oomor and led us to the fire in the middle of the clearing, where chunks of meat were roasting on sticks and brown circles of dough were piled on a stone at the edge of the coals.

"Just venison and acorn bread, I'm afraid. Bit of dried fruit from last summer stewed, but it'll fill the hole, eh, young lady and lad?"

Oomor sat with us long enough to eat some bread and fruit and then went off with Tem and Neema. "Kicklee farend," he said, grinning and patting the fat man's belly. We noticed that all the Neanderthals did that, as though it were good luck.

A young boy gave us each a stick of meat, and we helped ourselves to the acorn cakes and fruit. It tasted really good, and there was plenty of it, for a change.

"I'm glad they didn't kill those mammoths," I said, biting into a kebab. Quigley laughed.

"Oh, they never do," he said. "They get meat from the frozen carcasses in the winter sometimes, and very tasty it is too, but only the oldest men in the village can remember a successful hunt. It's more of a ritual, you know; if mammoths come, can spring be far behind? Ha ha, good one, if I do say."

The boy kept giving Quigley more and more food. He ate every bite and washed it all down with milk. He said something to the boy, who brought us a gourdful, setting it down and backing away quickly, as though he were afraid.

"Mare's milk," said Quigley. "Daresay it'd make decent cheese, if I knew anything about cheese making." He sighed and belched loudly. "Ah well, no use crying over spilt milk, eh? Ha ha! Now, let's have it kiddies. Tell the tale."

We told Quigley our story; sometimes Fig talked and sometimes I did. I finished by telling him we had decided to stay unless we could figure out how to go back on our own, because we didn't want Oomor to die. Quigley mopped his eyes with the raggedy necktie. Then he blew his nose on a large leaf, examined the result, and tossed it in the fire.

"Good lord. Most affecting, I must say. However, don't give up hope, young 'uns. Where there's a will, never say die, nihil desperandum and all that. Have to do a bit of thinking, cogitation, use the old noodle. In the meantime get some sleep, knits up the ravelled whatchamacallit, eh?"

"Sleave of care," I said. Mim and I read *Macbeth* together last winter.

"What?"

"'Sleep that knits up the ravelled sleave of care,' It's from *Macbeth*. Shakespeare," I said.

"Oh. Right. Good heavens, just so! Arms of Morpheus, now I lay me down, and so on."

Oomor reappeared and led us to the central cave, where we curled up beside the fire.

"Do you think he means we might get home after all?" I asked Fig.

"I doubt it," he said. "He must've been here a while if Oomor picked up all that English. If he knows so much, why doesn't *he* go home? He's a pretty weird shaman, if that's what he is. Sort of . . . silly." He gave an enormous yawn.

He was. He was funny looking and silly but there was something about him that made me feel better. I wondered what he was doing there, in that time and place, and as I wondered I fell asleep to the sound of my brother's snoring and the glow of Oomor's eyes shining through the shadows on the other side of the hearth.

FIG'S NOTEBOOK

JANUARY 20

We've been here a month. I have to conserve paper and my pen till I can invent more. If I can't figure this out, we'll have to stay here, like Q. He looks pretty healthy, and he's been here ninety years, so maybe after a while you get used to it.

Maybe Q's okay because he's already an adult so he's not growing anymore. How did he get here? Maybe it isn't the spinning but something else?

We have to go home. I have to think.

CHAPTER SIXTEEN

I AWOKE NEXT MORNING TO FIND WE WERE ALONE, lying under animal skins on a pile of pine branches. The branches smelled good, but they were prickly, so I sat up. The fire had died down and the air on my face was cold outside my fur cocoon. When I heard people moving around outside, I shook my brother, who groaned and pulled the furs over his head.

"Five minutes more, okay Beej?" he said. I shook him again and he struck at me with his fists until he remembered where we were and got up. I went to the cave entrance and looked out to see Oomor's mother and two of the other women standing in the river, holding pointed sticks and staring into the water. Every so often there was a splash as one of them speared a fish. Four of the hunters from the day before sat cross-legged on the bank, sharpening spears, while a fifth was skinning one deer beside a second bloody carcass. The two youngest hunters, a boy and a girl, were skinning and cleaning a pile of small dead animals—rabbits, squirrels, and birds—so it looked like there would be plenty of meat for the feast even without mammoth. I had to look away when the boy popped a rabbit's eye into his mouth and licked his fingers. I couldn't see Oomor or Quigley anywhere, so I waited just inside the cave entrance. Fig came up beside me, yawning.

Just then Oomor and Quigley walked into the camp. Oomor carried a huge armful of herbs and flowers, his face just visible above the pile.

"Aha!" said Quigley. "Bright-eyed and bushy-tailed, eh?" Oomor went into one of the caves with his pile, and Quigley headed toward the bank, where Neema was grilling fish over the fire. The fish smelled great. It was amazing to see how many Quigley ate, and even more amazing to hear how loudly he belched. Fig copied the belch, and I could see that if we did end up staying in the Ice Age, my brother was going to like it much better than me. He had a good scratch and leaned forward to poke the fire with a stick.

"Mr. Quigley," he said, "I don't understand how you got here and why you're not very old. You disappeared in 1910 and—"

"In 1913, young fella," said Quigley. "And I can't tell you how, exactly." Just then a flock of birds flew overhead, swirling like a banner against the early morning sky. One bird detached itself and swooped down to land on Quigley's shoulder. He chuckled and held out a handful of crumbs for Kero to eat.

"An exaltation," he said. "That's what it's called, you know, an exaltation of larks, when you see a flock of them like that. Clever little chap. Now, what was it? Oh, yes, time." He took off his necktie, gave it a half twist, and set it on the ground in a circle with its two ends touching.

"Run your finger over the outside without lifting it," he said. I did, even though it was covered with paint smears and food spots and was pretty disgusting. Of course my finger traced both inside and outside the circle.

"Mobius strip," said Fig. "Pa showed us that. So what?"

Quigley looked disappointed. "Good lord! Sharp as tacks, you two. Well, I can't say I understand it myself, but my friend Einstein said—"

"Wait a minute!" said Fig, "Einstein? You mean *Albert* Einstein?"

"Yes, that's the fellow. We used to eat sausages for breakfast and talk about time travel."

Fig's face was bright red, and he was spluttering with excitement. Quigley was staring into space, probably thinking about sausages. I got his attention by handing him my last butter rum LifeSaver.

"Mr. Quigley, maybe you better tell us your story and then please, if you know how, maybe you could help us get home? Without hurting Oomor?"

Quigley crunched up the LifeSaver happily, sucking on his teeth for a long time to get the last bits.

"Very nice indeed, missy, and much obliged. Cup of coffee would hit the spot just now, eh? Ah well. Let's see. . . .

"I was a painter, you know, a pretty good one; landscapes, animals, that sort of thing. Can't do people at all, never could, and that's where the money is, of course, portraits. So it was a fine thing for Hieronymous Quigley when I got the job painting dioramas at the museum. Very interesting work, tricky perspectives, travel expenses included, within reason. Within reason—aye, there's the rub, eh? I had to do a good bit of traveling to get the landscapes right, you see.

"I was on a tour of Northern Europe, sketching, when I met Albert in Zurich, in a café. He recommended the Kirschtorte, and we got to talking. My, it was fine, that torte—apricot jam, cream, toasted almonds . . . Where was I? Oh yes. Well, I didn't understand a tenth of what he was saying, you know, but we got on nonetheless. We met again in Prague and Berlin to eat and talk. As I say, his science jabber was way over my head, but it gave me ideas, I can tell you! I used to have some very odd dreams after a dinner with Albert, though it could have been the third slice of torte.

"It was when I went home that the trouble started. I have to admit, I'm not much of one for hiking, forests, countryside—all that Boy Scout stuff. I did plenty of sketching, you know, but it's perfectly true I spent some time in the cities—London, Budapest, Paris, Lyon—and a man has to have decent grub to keep his strength up, eh? Well, as I said, expenses within reason, and Mr. Hawes at the museum said mine were not. A good fellow, and he did what he could, but what with one thing and another I was left with considerable debts, and the creditors were after me. It wore me to a frazzle, I can tell you! Affected my appetite—a terrible thing that, when a man can't relish his victuals. Well, there I was one day, just putting the last touches on the lynx diorama and wonder ing how I would pay my landlady, not to mention my tailor and the bill at Luchow's. I had stepped out of the frame to get a good gander at the whole thing from a distance, when I heard voices. Someone was saying my name in an angry voice and Mr. Hawes's voice was arguing back.

"I suppose I panicked. I was a bit dizzy, you know, hadn't eaten more than a bite of breakfast, and I just ran. There was nowhere to go, the voices were coming closer and closer, and without thinking I jumped—straight into the diorama.

"You young'uns can guess what happened. Instead of landing on a wooden floor, I found myself swirling through a cold mist to land in the middle of this very village. I appeared smack in the ashes of the hearth outside the central cave. The ashes were still hot, and I can tell you I hopped out of there pretty fast! I was a good deal more surprised than these folk were. It seemed their shaman had died the day before and I showed up in the ashes of her funeral pyre, right on schedule according to Neema. Usually their shamans are women—women with blue eyes. But it so happened that at this particular time there weren't any blue-eyed women in the village, nor girls either. The only blue-eye was Oomor, who was only a kid, and here was Hieronymous Quigley, blue-eyed as you please, showing up like magic in the very ashes of old Heteba.

"So there I was, out of the frying pan, into the fire, as you might say. Ha ha, good one, that. I'm no shaman, heaven knows, but they seemed quite pleased. They find my clothes quite astonishing, and my pocketknife as well. I've always regretted that I'd been forced by circumstance to pawn my watch; now that would've surprised 'em! They especially like my, er . . . stoutness. They don't see much of that, you know, food not always plentiful hereabouts. That's it, really. I've been here seven years by my reckoning and—"

"Seven?" said Fig, "But you disappeared in 1913 and now it's 2003. You've been gone ninety years, not seven!"

Quigley looked at my brother with his bright blue eyes for a long moment before he answered.

"It's 2003, is it? Look around you, young fella, and tell me what year it is. And then tell me what 'now' means."

Fig stared back at Quigley and then ran his finger over the Mobius strip necktie, scowling like he does when he's thinking hard. Quigley went on with his story.

"Where was I? Oh yes, well here I was with this shaman job, not my line exactly. Made me nervous at first, you know, thinking that if I slipped up they might get a bit peevish. But very forgiving they are, and with Neema giving me a hand with potions and rituals, medicinal plants, that sort of thing, I've done all right. Then there's my drawing and painting, they've never seen anything like it. All they had were the handprints with charcoal and spit, and a few charcoal squiggles. I used to grind my own colors back in New York, and I've worked out some dandy paints with grease and ground minerals. I've taught young Oomor; he has a real knack for it—and he's quite extraordinary with the mind-reading business to boot, as you've already seen. Now that's taken some getting used to, I can tell you! I'm not too swift at it myself, I'm afraid, but I've learned their lingo and taught 'em a bit of mine. All in all it's not too bad. I miss things of course . . . food mostly. I don't suppose you have any more of those sweets, do you, missy?"

I shook my head, and he sighed.

"You don't need to worry about getting us home, Mr. Quigley," I said. I thought it might make him feel better since I didn't have any more LifeSavers. Instead he looked terrified.

"Oh dear, oh dear; that's just it. Sat up half the night with Oomor, trying to find a way, cogitating, and really, I just don't see . . . young fella is stuck on it no matter what I say. You must convince him—very dangerous this time travel thing. Look at old Heteba, she—" He stopped suddenly.

"What do you mean?" asked Fig. "What about her?"

"Oh, now I've done it. Cat out of the bag, oh blast!" He mopped his face with the necktie, adding a streak of yellow paint to his nose.

"Well, she died, you see," he said. "She was going into the dream place, as they call it, spinning you know, gray mist. She vanished, and when she came back, she was dead."

Fig had gone very pale. It's like looking into a mirror if you're a twin, and I knew my face must look the same.

"But wasn't she old?" I asked.

"Oh yes, there's that of course. She was also . . ." He looked sick. "She was, er . . . injured."

"Like us when we went back too far," said Fig. "When we almost . . ."

"Precisely," said Quigley. He stared gloomily into the fire.

Oomor came back just then and pulled Quigley aside. They stood by the river, and I had the feeling they were arguing, though it was an odd sort of argument since they weren't doing much talking. Quigley massaged one side of his head as though it hurt him, and once I heard him say, "But they don't *want* . . ." After a while he disappeared into the central cave, leaving us alone by the fire.

FIG'S NOTEBOOK

JANUARY 21

Einstein! I'm talking with a guy who knew Einstein, and all he learned was the Mobius strip! He didn't spin, so it's not that. It must be something else. Being dizzy? Dizzy and what? I still think spinning comes into it somehow. Spinning. The earth is spinning, our galaxy is spinning, the whole universe is spinning in space. Is space spinning? Can nothing be spinning? Is space nothing? Is time spinning? I wish I had my books.

FACTS	QUESTIONS
1. We traveled from 2003 to 1913.	1. What year is it here?
2. Q traveled from 1913.	2. Are we still in France?
3. Ms. Jobe was from 1913.	
4. 2003−1913=90 years.	
5. A & I spun both times.	
6. Q didn't spin.	
7. We were all dizzy.	
8. We all came through the diorama the first time.	

CHAPTER SEVENTEEN

"**T**HERE'S NO WAY WE'RE GOING," I SAID. "OOMOR can't make us." Fig was scribbling in his notebook and didn't seem to hear. I wondered what he'd do when his pen ran out of ink and there was no more paper. I could smell him, and myself too, even sitting outdoors by the fire with other smells all around. I noticed that Quigley smelled okay, and he'd been there seven years, so he must have had some way of washing. He doesn't seem like the cold bath type. I was just thinking I'd ask him when Fig stopped writing and said, "I think I've figured it out, Al. Look."

I looked at his notebook, where he'd drawn a lot of circles with stick figures and arrows labeled A, B, C, and so on. He's a terrible drawer; the stick figures looked like bugs.

"Oh, that's just great, Fig; clear as mud."

"No, listen, I think I understand, it's like a merry-go-round."

"What is? What are you talking about?"

"Time, of course. There's a word for it: *paradox.* That's why it's all mixed up, why Quigley has been here seven of his years and ninety of ours, why we landed in 1913 with Mary Jobe, why we went back to the beginning of things and almost—"

"Don't say it!" I got up to go but he pulled me back down.

"Fig," I said, "what difference does it make? We're stuck here, and I don't think Quigley can do anything, whatever Oomor says."

"I don't either, that's not the point. You know how at the merry-go-round in the park you can jump on when it's moving, and before you jump it seems to be spinning, but once you're on, it's the world that's going round?"

"Yeah, so?"

"Well, the thing is that they're *both* spinning, everything is: the earth, the universe, everything. Maybe that's what time is, a lot of merry-go-rounds. Maybe, if you jump at just the right time, you can go from your own merry-go-round to another one. Mary Jobe was in 1913 and Quigley came here in 1913. Maybe in some years or some places the merry-go-rounds are closer together so you can jump from one to another. That other shaman, she must have jumped at the wrong time."

"You mean, if we could figure out when to catch it, we'd go back to our own time?"

"Eggzackly!" He sat back, looking pleased with himself.

"So, Einstein, just how do we do *that?*"

Just then Quigley came out of the cave. He was wearing a

raggedy black suit and a shirt that looked as though it had been white a long time ago. He still had on the necktie and boots and an even gloomier expression than before. Oomor was dancing around and pulling him toward us. His excitement made a bright fizzing in my brain, like a Fourth of July sparkler, as Kero hovered just over our heads, singing.

"Kicklee!" Oomor cried. "Kicklee home Nyooyawk!" He practically dragged us over to Quigley, who reminded me of the picture of Eeyore in *The House at Pooh Corner*. Even his belly seemed to droop.

"It's really not half bad here, you know," he said. "You two would probably get used to it. I have." He sounded as though he didn't believe himself, and I wondered if he felt as wrong in this time as we did.

"We already told you, we're not going. We don't want Oomor to die," I said.

"Just so! I've tried to tell him, but he won't listen. Stubborn boy."

Oomor laughed, sending mind-sparklers everywhere. It tickled, and I couldn't help smiling. He led us toward the caves with Quigley trailing behind. The other Neanderthals stood still and quiet, watching as we passed. We came to a small hole in the cliffside, less than two feet wide, and halted as Oomor's mother stepped forward. She touched his face and hugged him, handing him a bag of acorn cakes, whispering his name over and over. She looked so sad and scared I wished I could explain to her that she didn't need to worry, we weren't going. I started to send a mind-picture when suddenly I felt my brain explode and heard a terrible scream. Neema fell to the ground and the rest of the villagers staggered around, howling with pain, blood trickling from their noses.

I thought my head would split open, and I shut my eyes to block the flashing lights. "Too loud! Hurts!" I gasped.

"*You* tell her then!" shouted Fig. "Tell her not to be afraid; we're not going."

I tried, but the pain was too bad, and I couldn't focus. Oomor was the only one not holding his head. A picture of Mim, thin and white in her hospital bed, formed in my mind, and as I watched, her eyes opened and she looked right at us. "Come home," she said. "Come home," and she disappeared as we reached out to touch her.

"Mutta, Mutta Mim," said Oomor, taking our hands and pulling us toward the cave. Quigley's face was greenish white. I felt sick, and Fig shook his head furiously.

"We can't go! We don't know how it works. Tell him we need more time!" I tried again, taking Oomor's hand to make the mind-pictures clearer. I thought about Dreidel Boy and about Oomor as he was now, alive and real. I pictured us laughing in the meadow, sharing mare's milk, singing together by the fire, trying to show him that he mustn't die, not even to send us home. I had to focus my whole mind and stay relaxed at the same time, and when I finished, I was out of breath, like I'd run a race. Oomor just smiled at me while the other Neanderthals crowded around, patting me and murmuring. Oomor's mother wiped the blood from her nose and took Fig's head in her hands, shaking it gently. "Ah Bah Feek, Ah Bah Oomor," she said, laughing. The people grew quiet again, as though they were waiting for something to happen. I can't read their thoughts clearly, but I can see my brother and me through their eyes. We were magical creatures who came with the earthquake, just before the spring feast, and even though the mammoth was lost, the village was safe, and no one was hurt. Now they expected us to go back to the spirit world, taking Oomor with us to follow his dream. Every shaman had to make that journey, and they didn't always come back alive.

Quigley's face had returned to its normal pink color. He wiped his bloody nose on his necktie and said, "Steady there, young fella, you pack quite a wallop. No use arguing, you know. He's made up his mind to go, with you or without."

Oomor said, "Feek, Ah-lee, Kicklee home," and pulled us toward the cave.

"What does he mean?" asked Fig, trying to pull away.

"I don't know," I said. "But I'm not going in there; they can't make us."

Oomor tugged at our hands but we dug in our heels, and Fig got the look on his face that Bijou calls "hog stubborn." At last Oomor let go and stepped back. Kero landed on his shoulder.

"Kero, Oomor, Mutta," he said, "*Ah Bah* Mutta!" Kero fluttered into the opening of the cave, and Oomor knelt and crawled in after the little bird, his feet disappearing into the darkness. We watched as Quigley stepped toward the entrance.

"Come along, young'uns," he said. "Screw your courage to the sticking place, eh?"

All I could see was that narrow cave, like a black mouth that would swallow us up forever, and the look of horror on Quigley's face when he'd talked about the old shaman. Was it friendship holding me back, or fear?

Suddenly I remembered standing with Bijou at Quarry Lake in Maine, our toes curled over the ledge, looking at the dark surface far below. It was our first swim of the season. Bijou grabbed my hand.

"Sometimes you just have to take a chance and LEAP!" she said, so we yelled blue murder and jumped, sending a fountain of icy water into the summer sky.

"Fig," I said, "we have to take the chance." He just stood there, looking sick. I hesitated another minute and then called to Oomor, "Wait, I'm coming too!" and I ducked in. Fig yelled, "Allie!" and though I answered him, I don't think he heard me because he kept calling my name. I couldn't hear Oomor up ahead, and I couldn't turn around. My brother's voice echoed behind me. "Feet! I can smell your feet!"

"Don't push!" I said.

We crawled farther and farther into the tunnel until suddenly the passage took a turn to the right, and I lost all sense of direction. I wasn't sure if the sounds I heard were the others or some slimy cave creature, and it was so dark it didn't matter whether my eyes were open or shut. It didn't help to feel around with my hands, and I was afraid I would touch something creepy, so I just kept crawling forward. The tunnel got so narrow I had to get down on my belly and wriggle along on my elbows, and the darkness was damp and thick against my face. I thought of all the rocks and dirt pressing us down and down. I couldn't breathe. I was choking! Something was panting, some animal. I tried to move, to turn around; I wanted to scream and scream and scream . . . Then I heard Quigley.

"Tiddum pum pum tiddum, pa-dum pa-dum pa-dum, tiddum tiddum tiddum . . . Oh, drat; there goes a button. Blasted boy, stubborn as a mule. Very tight fit, this, must cut back on the grub . . ." I began to breathe more normally. The tune he was humming sounded familiar, and I wondered what it was.

At last I felt a cool breeze and heard Oomor scrambling to stand up. We seemed to have reached an open space, though I still couldn't see. There was a grunt and a loud pop, like a cork coming out of a bottle, as Quigley scrambled out of the passage in front of me. Then my head and shoulders were free, and I climbed out as Fig came up behind me. I heard the click of firestones and saw sparks grow into a yellow flame that lit Oomor's face as he fed branches into the fire from a pile near the hearth. The flames grew till we could see the enormous cave almost to its ceiling. Stalagmites and stalactites sparkled pink, white, green, and gold in the firelight and water trickled in the distance with a sound like tiny bells. Along the walls wolves, mammoths, deer, lions, and horses galloped and hunted in black, red, yellow, and white.

"Oh!" I gasped. "It's beautiful! It's like a cathedral!"

"All our own work, and much obliged, young lady," said Quigley. "Well, except for the little mother goddess, of course. Nobody knows who made her. Actually Oomor did most of the animals, and very fine, they are."

I looked at the hearth. It was made of flat rocks set in a circle and carved with pictures of plants and animals. On one side stood a smooth gray geode stone, split open and lined with purple jewels like the ones at the museum. A small ivory statue stood inside. She had a crown of braided hair and big hips and bosoms just like the woman Oomor had drawn in his cave, and I could tell she was much older than Quigley's paintings.

"Ah Bah Mutta," said Oomor, and he sat down behind the statue, Kero perched on his head, preening himself after the flight through the tunnel. We sat down on either side of them. Quigley looked very uncomfortable opposite Oomor. Oomor's face seemed to float in the firelight just above the ivory goddess. He held his hand out to me as though he wanted something. I didn't understand, and then I remembered the song Quigley was humming in the tunnel and something clicked into place, like a piece of a jigsaw puzzle. I reached into my pocket and felt the dreidel at the very bottom. I held it in my fist, remembering what Mim said when she gave it to me. "It spins just like the earth, Allie Bee," she said. "You have the whole world in your hand!" I took it out slowly and stared at it, feeling the heat of the fire on my face. I began to sing the song Mim taught me; the words came into my mind like a dream from another time.

> "I have a little dreidel,
> I made it out of clay,
> And when it's dry and ready,
> Dreidel I will play."

"That's the ticket!" said Quigley. "Good tune. My landlady used to sing it to her children. Fine woman, made splendid coffeecakes, you know. With nuts." He hummed along in a buzzy voice, and soon Oomor and Fig joined in, our voices making strange echoes against the high walls of the cave. When the song ended, I set the point of the dreidel on the hearthstone and gave it a twirl. It wobbled for a moment then began to spin.

Quigley stood up. "Not at all sure about this," he said. "Could be dangerous, risky—very."

"Ah-lee, Feek. Home?" said Oomor, holding a hand out to each of us. I looked at Fig, and he looked back at me across the fire.

"Take a chance?" I asked.

"And leap!" he said. He took a deep breath.

"Hand!" said Fig as he reached out to Oomor.

"Hahnd!" said Oomor, and he pulled us to our feet as Quigley took our other hands to form a ring around the hearth. The dreidel still spun in the middle. It was odd that it would keep on so long without slowing down. In fact, it seemed to speed up. Oomor smiled and said, "Ah-lee, Feek, Kicklee. Mutta Mim home!" He tugged my hand to start us circling round the fire.

"It's the merry-go-round!" said Fig. "It is, isn't it? We're going to jump on!"

"I think so. I don't know. Oh, Fig!"

"Allie!" my brother called as Quigley and Oomor pulled us round and round, faster and faster.

"Here we go, kiddies! Can't stop now, time flies, seize the day and so forth!"

"Mr. Quigley, please! Will he die?" I was getting dizzy.

"Don't know!" he said, panting. "That last shaman, Heteba—oh dear, giddiness, quite sickening!"

We were moving so fast that the cave seemed to spin around us, the animals on the walls racing past in a blur of hooves and horns. All I could see clearly was the little ivory goddess and the dreidel spinning on the hearthstone before her.

We spun faster and faster, until the gray mist began to rise around us, turning, turning.

"Now!" said Quigley.

"JUMP!" cried Oomor.

"All aboooaaarrrrrd!" cried Quigley, and we jumped and the mist caught us and spun us away into the swirling, twirling, vast and whirling world.

FIG'S NOTEBOOK

JANUARY 22

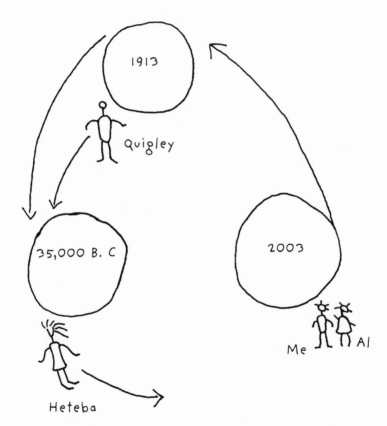

CHAPTER EIGHTEEN

THE FOG WRAPPED ITS SOFT GRAY ARMS AROUND us as we spun, hand in hand, round and round. I couldn't tell if it was Oomor's fire we saw through the mist or the flames of a burning Earth. Were we moving forward in time or back again into the past? Just before the cave vanished altogether the little goddess changed till it was Neema's face under the braided crown. The face grew longer and thinner, the ivory braids turning to flame-colored curls as Fig cried out, "Mim!" and I saw our mother's face shining in the firelight. Then the bright curls grew long, swirling above her head, and the last thing I saw was Bijou smiling through the mist as the cave disappeared.

The spinning slowed, the fog grew thinner until we seemed to be hanging in the air. As the dizziness passed we saw where we were: floating three feet above the floor of the little room next to the Hall of European Mammals in the American

Museum of Natural History in New York City. We were home! Only we were there and not there at the same time, and it made me feel airsick. Oomor's eyes were as big as anything, and he was so excited he was bouncing up and down. He looked at us and shouted with surprise, and we looked back at him. We were all half invisible; we could see right through each other as though we were made of smoke; when I looked at my hand holding on to Oomor's, it was smoky too.

I turned to look at my brother and was surprised to see him staring at the wall behind me, his eyes practically bugging out of his head. I turned to look and saw an arm. Just that, an arm, sticking out of the wall and flapping horribly; the hand reached out with blind, wiggling fingers.

"It's Quigley!" said Fig in a strangled voice. "He's stuck!" It was Quigley's hand, not very clean, and the arm was dressed in a raggedy black coat sleeve.

"Kicklee!" cried Oomor, seizing his hand. He pulled, and Quigley's head and other arm came through the wall, but no matter how hard we tugged, the rest of him stayed stuck.

"Oh, drat!" said the head, and I was very relieved to see that he seemed to be all right. In *Star Trek,* when someone gets stuck in the transporter, they come through all mangled and bloody.

"Wha . . . what's happening?" asked Fig.

"Stuck, blast it! My hindquarters in the past, my front in the future, ow!" Quigley wriggled and thrashed but the wall held him tight.

"Are you all right?" I asked, wondering how and where the rest of him was.

"Trapped, young lady. 'The whirligig of time brings in his revenges' eh? 'Oh that this too too solid flesh would melt,' dammit! Oh, sorry, bad language, no call for—oh blast!"

Then I noticed that Quigley was sticking out of the wall right over a glass display case. Even though I couldn't see into it from where I was, I knew what was there: Oomor's bones. But Oomor was right here, floating in the air beside me! His hand felt warm and solid even though it was transparent, and he was still pulling on Quigley with the other hand, saying, "Kicklee! Kicklee!"

"All right, old son, no need to . . . *ouch!* Hold on, hold on there! What a pickle, eh?"

Just then the dreidel appeared over my head, spinning more and more slowly, wobbling the way a top does when it's about to stop.

Suddenly I knew there was no time to waste. I gave Oomor a shove.

"Oomor, you have to go now, you and Quigley! JUMP!"

"That's the ticket, young lady! Come on m'boy!" said Quigley.

"Kicklee home!" said Oomor, yanking hard on Quigley's arm.

"No, no, my boy; this isn't home for me. Not my time, don't you see? Oh, *ouch,* stop it! Tell him, missy, this time is neither mine nor his; we have to go *now.*" Fig and I tried to talk to Oomor but he wouldn't listen, he was so sure Quigley belonged here with us.

"Oh, Mr. Quigley, it's slowing down, you have to go!" The

dreidel was hardly moving now. Suddenly Quigley grabbed Oomor by the front of his fur tunic. He drew himself up as well as he could while sticking out of the wall, and he no longer looked the least bit silly.

"AH BAH QUIGLEY!" he shouted in a voice like a lion's roar. "AH BAH MUTTA-RAH *NAX!*" Oomor looked startled and stopped pulling on Quigley's arm.

"Kicklee, nax muttah-rah," he said, bowing and touching his forehead to Quigley's hand. Then he put the bag of fire-stones into my hand, and I felt a flash in my head as he let go and leapt into the air, still holding on to Quigley. I shut my eyes so as not to see his head slam into the wall.

I waited but there was no sound of a crash, so I opened my eyes. Oomor and Quigley were gone, and my brother was again staring at the smooth white wall with his mouth open.

"Where'd they go?" I asked him.

"They just turned into fog and disappeared into the wall," he said. "Swirling, like water going down a drain. And look," He pointed, and there on top of the glass case were Oomor's bone flute and skin bag. The dreidel had disappeared. I noticed that Fig's hand looked completely solid. Before I could speak we fell through the air and landed with a hard bump on the marble floor. I sat up and rubbed my elbow to take away the buzzing in my funny bone. There we were, sure enough, in the room of half-forgotten odds and ends that leads to the Hall of European Mammals, and there was the case that held . . . what? We got up and looked inside. There it was, just as we'd seen it a hundred times before. The skeleton lay on its back, arms folded, holding a large bead in its hand. The dreidel. We looked down at the heavy jaw and deep eye sockets of Oomor's skull.

I couldn't help it; I started to cry. I looked at my brother.

"We did our best, Al," he said in a froggy voice, wiping his nose on his sleeve.

"It was all wasted." I sobbed.

"There you are! We looked everywhere; where have you been?"

It was Bijou, looking worried and rumpled and unbelievably dear. A tall man in a museum sweatshirt walked beside her. And there was Pa with—oh, it couldn't be! But it was! It was magic, a miracle: MIM! Her leg was in a cast and she was leaning on a crutch, hobbling along as fast as she could, but it was Mim—she was real; she was here! We yelled and ran to her so fast we almost knocked her over.

"Hey! Hold on there! What's this, a herd of rhinoceroses?" She laughed and struggled to keep her balance as we jumped around her, crying and trying to hug her, crutch and all.

"Thank goodness Freddy was working late or we'd never have gotten in. It's long past closing; we were worried to death!" said Bijou. She hugged us and we tried to hug her back without letting go of Mim. My eyes were so full of tears that her face looked all blurry.

"We missed you *so much!*" I said. Bijou grinned and rumpled my hair.

"Well, sure you did, ragamuffin. Eighteen hours without seeing the world's greatest aunt—that's gotta be rough!" She looked more closely at us and so did Mim, and I realized we must have looked pretty bad. Our clothes were scorched, filthy, and much too big; our faces were smeared with soot; and our hair was greasy and tangled.

"Oh my god, what's happened? Are you all right?" Mim pulled at us, feeling all over to make sure nothing was broken.

"We're fine, but Beej, we've been gone for weeks and weeks, since just before Christmas. How come—" Pa interrupted me.

"Look, you two, this is no time for jokes. We were really worried. You're old enough to know better than to wander off like that without telling us."

"But it's been over a month and we kept trying to get home and to change things so you wouldn't die and—"

The adults were all staring at Fig as though he had gone crazy, and he just stopped talking suddenly with his mouth wide open. Then he grabbed Mim again so hard she staggered and he just said her name over and over, butting his head against her and hanging on with both hands.

"How how how how how?" I said, pressing my face into the rough wool of Bijou's coat.

"Fig, Allie, calm down! It's okay, you're all right now," said Pa. He put his arms around us.

"It's not us, it's Mim—she's well! She's well!"

"Well, I will be if you rhinoceroses don't break my other leg," said Mim. I felt like I could just stand there forever, looking up at her dear, sweaty face. I knew I had a huge, dumb grin on my own face because I could see the same grin on Fig's. Mim began to laugh.

"Good lord, you two look like a real pair of hooligans!"

"And you smell terrible," said Bijou, wrinkling her nose.

"But how?" said Fig. He wiped his face on his sleeve, which made it look even worse.

"How'd we find you?" asked Bijou, twisting a lock of hair around her finger as she always does when she's puzzled. "Well, it was rather odd. Oliver and I had already searched the museum when you two didn't show up this afternoon, and we were thinking what to do next, whether to call the police. Mim was sitting by the phone, calling around, looking through her address book, humming to herself the way she does when she's concentrating. She was singing that silly song about the dreidel, when all of a sudden she dropped the book and said, 'They're at the museum, we have to go *now!*' She wouldn't listen to us or wait at home, she called Dr. Maldonado here to let us in, and she led us right to you, like a bloodhound. She's a witch; I always said so." Bijou grinned at her sister.

"It was a sort of brain flash," said Mim, adjusting her crutch. "I just *knew* you'd be in this room, by your Dreidel Boy. Oliver checked here before; where were you, anyway?"

Fig and I looked at each other. Out of the corner of my eye I saw Dr. Maldonado pick up the bag of firestones I had dropped when we saw Mim. He examined it, brushing his floppy black hair back with one hand. "Interesting workmanship," he muttered. "Bison hide? Don't think so, not Native American. Inuit perhaps?" He reached inside and pulled out the stones.

Bijou and Mim were asking us about our clothes and sounding more and more confused. We tried to explain but they kept interrupting to ask questions. Finally Fig lost his temper.

"The clothes don't matter! Will you just please listen?" He pulled at Bijou's arm, and after a moment she sat. Pa helped Mim to sit down too, with her cast sticking straight out in front of her and Fig and me on either side. We wanted to stay close to her so she wouldn't vanish. Pa hunkered down holding Mim's crutch, and Dr. Maldonado folded up his long legs like a stork. I guess a person who studies birds has to be very good at sitting still and listening.

Now that we had their full attention I realized how impossible our story would sound, and I could feel my face getting hot. Fig's was bright red.

"You tell," he muttered. So I took a deep breath and told it all, from Mim's coma to the final spinning journey out of the past and Oomor's body in the glass case. I choked up a couple of times but I kept on; I didn't care if it sounded wacko. My mother put her arm around me, wonderfully real and bony under the heavy cloth of her coat.

When I was done, the grownups sat quietly for a minute. At last Bijou spoke in a shaky voice.

"She *was* in a coma. For twenty-four hours after they got her out she was on a respirator. Oliver sat by her bed the whole time. We didn't think it was necessary to tell you; it would only have worried you more." She blew her nose into a Kleenex. Mim patted her hand but as she did, she was staring into space, the way Mim does when she's trying to figure something out.

"Time warp," she said thoughtfully. "Are you saying that a month in the Ice Age for you was eighteen hours for us, and ninety years were only seven for Quigley? So that for you I was still in the hospital in a coma? And when you changed the past, it changed the present so that for us I was at Bijou's with nothing worse than a broken leg? Is that possible? Of course we have no objective proof but . . ."

Dr. Maldonado took off his glasses and wiped them on his sweatshirt. Then he stood up without speaking and gestured to us to follow. Pa helped Mim to her feet, and we all walked out of the little room and into the Hall of European Mammals. Dr. Maldonado switched on the light, and there all around us were deer and bear, birds, foxes, badgers; all the creatures in their painted landscapes behind the glass.

"Lynx," he said.

And there they were, just as before, the same speckled, big-eared cats, lying around under the pines in the green light of the forest.

"She shot them after all," I said. "She lied to us!"

"That's not it, don't you get it? He's saying it never happened, that it was all a stupid dream," said Fig. I had just opened my mouth to argue when Dr. Maldonado grabbed us both and shoved us closer to the diorama.

"Sign!" he said. "Read it."

We stared at the big gold letters set into the wooden frame. *Lynx lynx* it said, just like always. Then we noticed the smaller black print underneath:

Hunted to near extinction before the First World War, the lynx has made a remarkable comeback, thanks to the pioneering work of the great conservationist and explorer Mary Jobe (later Mary Jobe Akeley

1886–1966). Still a protected species, the lynx is now a common sight in the forests of Northern Europe.
Collected by Layman Jameson 1912.

"A common sight," I said, touching the glass that felt so cool and solid and real.

"So it *did* happen!" said Fig. "I knew it, it's all in my notes—look." He pulled the tattered notebook out of his pocket.

"On the contrary; that's exactly what it said this afternoon," said Dr. Maldonado. "I noticed this exhibit particularly because that bird in the foreground is improperly labeled. It's not a greenish warbler, it's a chiffchaff. You must have incorporated the sign into your dream. Quite remarkable in a way, so much detail."

"But it wasn't a dream!" I said, banging on the glass with my fist. "It was *real*."

"Read my notes!" said Fig at the same time. "Come on, just look at them, why don't you?"

"Now, now," said Dr. Maldonado, looking rather nervous. "Dreams can seem very real, you know. People do all sorts of things in their sleep—walk, eat, write . . ."

"That's just it, Freddy," said Mim. "All that detail, how could they know all that, even with all the reading they do?" She put an arm around me. "Come on, Allie Bee, I want to have another look at your Neanderthal."

We turned away from the diorama and went back to the little room where Oomor lay. My brother and I stood staring into the case. All at once Fig bit his lip and turned away. I wrapped my arms around the end of the case near Oomor's head and rested my cheek on the glass. Mim stroked my hair.

"He's right, you know. We don't have any real proof."

"We know what we know," I said. "Things *have* changed."

Mim sighed. Bijou was staring at me with a puzzled look on her face. She touched my head.

"Your hair," she said. "Your hair is different." She turned to Mim. "I wanted her to get a decent haircut, remember? I said to you this morning we should go to Mr. LoMonaco. Now it looks . . . it seems longer. And you're both definitely thinner." She cupped my face in her hand.

"Changed!" said Fig, grabbing my arm. "That's it, Al! Things are different because we *did* change the past, but they can't see it because they stayed on their own merry-go-round. Our hair and the dirt, that's all they can see that's different."

"A paradox of time," said Mim. "I wonder . . ."

Dr. Maldonado was staring down into the case and muttering. Mim and Pa like all good scientists are always curious, so they joined him, and looked closely at the bones. They talked together for a few minutes and then turned to us.

"Allie, look here; you too Fig." I didn't want to, but as Pa spoke we did look, and we listened hard.

"See the size of the skull in proportion to the rest?" he said, pointing. "And the way the teeth are worn? Look at those finger joints and knees, how deformed they are. That's arthritis. Look at the bones of the left arm, see? They've been broken and mended." Pa looked at us expectantly. "Don't you see," said Mim. "These are the bones of an old man, a full grown Neanderthal, not a child. He was probably over forty when he died, which would have been very old in those days."

We looked down at the bones.

"You mean he didn't die when he brought us home?" asked Fig, his face lighting up. "He went back to his own time and grew up?"

"Could be," said Mim.

"He got old!" I said in amazement, looking at the dark bones. "But what about Quigley?"

Nobody answered. Nobody knew.

CHAPTER NINETEEN

I LOOKED AT MY MOTHER, AND FATHER, AND MY AUNT. I could see they wanted to believe the story, strange as it was. I pushed my head into Bijou's hand like a cat and remembered that what I'd missed in the past was not museums and movies and hamburgers (well, I *did* miss hamburgers) but Bijou and Mim and Pa. Mim put her arms around us, balancing on her good leg.

"Remember how the cicadas fly away at the end of summer on their brand new wings and leave their dried-up old husks stuck to the trunk of the maple tree?" she said. "That's what's in that case; just Oomor's husk. He did what he meant to do; he followed his dream. It's the best, the bravest, the most important thing anyone can do, and he couldn't have done it without you. Your friend was very brave and very wise," she said.

"Well," said Bijou, "Time travel or not, you two are grubby!" She tried to wipe some of the dirt off with her scarf but it didn't do much good and probably ruined the scarf. We were covered with, as Fig pointed out, thirty-five thousand years of dirt, so it would take more than a scarf to clean us up.

"A hot shower, or maybe two, and dinner," said Mim. "Let's go."

"No acorns," said Fig.

"No bugs!" I said.

"Steaks!" said Pa, taking our hands and waltzing us around the marble floor. "Steaks a foot thick and ice cream from Gabriel's!"

"Peanut butter fudge ripple," said Fig. "What did Tarzan say when he saw the elephants coming?"

"Here come the elephants!" shouted Mim, Pa, Bijou, and me all together. Dr. Maldonado looked puzzled and handed me the skin bag. "These are firestones, you know, for making fire."

I smiled at him. "I know," I said.

Fig and I took a moment to touch the case where our friend lay, to say thank you.

"Allie, look," said my brother. He bent over and picked up something from behind the case. It was a silk necktie in a red and blue pattern, very dirty. "Quigley!" I said.

"Do you think he got back to his own time?" We stared at the tie but found no answer. Fig put it in his pocket, and we all walked out of the room through the corridors of the old museum, with Dr. Maldonado trailing behind.

"Hang on," said Pa as we walked past a water fountain with a public telephone beside it. "I want to call Thad. He's been waiting by the phone at Yellow House in case you guys called there." He walked over to the telephone, fumbling in his pocket for change, and leaving Fig and me staring after him with our mouths open.

"Thad," said Fig.

"That's right, cookie," said Bijou. "He's joining us all for Christmas, with Susie and both of the boys."

"*Uncle* Thad?" I said. "Pa's brother?"

"Yes, of course, who else? What's the matter with . . ."

"Oliver says calloo callay! and he's going to make hot fudge sauce on condition that you tell him the whole story," said Pa, coming back with a big grin on his face. We walked on toward the exit, Fig and I following a little behind the grownups, wondering what it would be like to meet Uncle Thad and Susie and the boys.

"It must be his wife and children," Fig said.

"They're our cousins, Fig. We created our own cousins!"

"Not created," he said. "We just sort of . . . made them possible. But what else have we changed, Al?" His face looked scared. I knew what he meant, and for a minute I know my face mirrored his. I gulped.

"I guess we'll find out," I said. I could see Fig chewing on that thought for a while, the way he does. But I didn't have any room, any *time* to be scared anymore because there were Mim and Pa and Beej right in front of us, laughing and talking with Dr. Maldonado, as real as . . .

"As real as *them*," said Fig, his face breaking into a big goofy grin. "As Pa and . . . the Muttas!"

"Mutta Mim, Mutta Bijou," I said.

"Eggzackly."

"Hey, you two," said Mim. "What's all this dawdling? Come on, give your gimpy old mother a hand." We walked between her and Bijou. Mim leaned on Fig's shoulder and Bijou wound her arm around mine. I turned my head to breathe in the scent of Joy perfume on her wrist.

"You smell good," I said, putting my arm around her waist.

Pa strode ahead with Dr. Maldonado, talking and gesturing with his arms. ". . . paleontologists, you see, simply *extrapolate* from completely insufficient . . ." I caught Fig's eye and he grinned.

It was spooky to be in the museum so long after closing, with most of the lights out and our footsteps echoing on the stone floor. Spooky in a good way, like when there's a storm outside and you're all safe and warm by the fire. In a few days we'll leave for Yellow House to spend Christmas as we always do, only this year we'll meet the Uncle Thad we've always wondered about and a new aunt and two new cousins. We'll cut down a tree from our own woods, and Pa will make his horrible cranberry, horseradish, and sour cream relish. It's the color of Pepto-Bismol and nobody likes it, but we say it's delicious and hide it under the turkey bones. Bijou and Mim will fill the house with good baking smells, and Pie will race around knocking things over and crashing into piles of wrapping paper. On Christmas Eve we'll go out caroling, and Pa will round up everybody who has no place to go for Christmas and invite them all to dinner. I thought I'd ask my parents if Dr. Maldonado could come. I noticed he wasn't wearing any socks, and there was a big grease stain on his sweatshirt, so I thought he might not have much of a social life. Fig grabbed my hand and whispered, "Let's ask Pa to invite Dr. Maldonado, okay?" Did he read my mind? I thought I'd try some telepathy again later, when I wasn't so hungry.

We went through the rotunda, past the barosaurus and its baby, out the doors, and onto the top step. It was late, and there was no one on Central Park West, though the sounds of the city hummed and roared all around us. New York seemed very loud after the Ice Age. Then, through the noise of traffic on Columbus Avenue, we heard the high, glorious sound of a bird singing.

"What?" said Dr. Maldonado, craning his head so far forward it seemed he would tumble down the steps. He peered into the moonlight with his sharp bird-watcher's eyes. "There!" he said and pointed to the sculpture group at the foot of the stairs.

A little brown bird swooped back and forth in the light of a nearby streetlamp, singing its heart out. It landed on Teddy Roosevelt's head and looked up at us for a moment before it took off into the night.

"*Alauda arvensis*—my goodness! Most unusual, especially at night, in winter; first sighting in North America perhaps?" mumbled Dr. Maldonado, scribbling in a small notebook.

We followed the flight of the little bird as it rose against the sky, singing as though its voice could light the world.

"Skylark," said Dr. Maldonado, trying to be helpful. "Strictly European bird, very unusual in these parts. Blown in by a storm perhaps." He grinned down at us happily.

Fig and I grinned back because he was such a nice man. But we knew what bird it was, and we watched Kero's flight as long as we could, until he disappeared into the starry sky. I think Mim and Pa and Bijou knew too.

"An exaltation of *us*," I said. And we all walked together, out of the old museum into the sparkling winter night.

AUTHOR'S NOTES

MARY JOBE

Timespinners is fiction. However, some things in this book are based on fact. All of the characters are imaginary except for Mary Jobe, who was a famous educator and explorer. A high peak in the Canadian Rockies was named Mount Jobe in her honor. In 1924 she married the wildlife artist and adventurer Carl Akeley, whose name can be found on exhibits all over the American Museum of Natural History or in any encyclopedia. Like most women of her time, she took her husband's name and dedicated herself to his work, so the only place you will find Mary Jobe's name is in a wonderful book called *Dinosaurs in the Attic* by Douglas Preston.

LYNX

There is no Hall of European Mammals at the American Museum of Natural History, but you can see a close cousin of *Lynx lynx* in the Hall of North American Mammals. Some conservation groups are attempting to reintroduce the lynx into parts of northern Europe, but their efforts have been frustrated by the destruction of habitat caused by increasing human population, the opposition of local farmers, and the fur trade's continuing slaughter of these rare and beautiful animals for the sake of fashion. You can find more information about lynxes through www.lynx.uio.no.

Neanderthals

There are many unanswered questions about Neanderthals. They buried their dead with some ceremony, and their stone tools were efficient and beautiful, but nobody knows whether they spoke a language or created art, or why and how they disappeared. Some scientists think that they were killed or outwitted by our ancestors the Cro-Magnons; some think the two groups interbred. In *Timespinners* I chose to assume that the "Ah Bah," the blue-eyed ones (or spirits, as Oomor's tribe sees them), were the offspring of encounters between Neanderthal women and Cro-Magnon men. Oomor's artistic talent and his hunger for "words and more words" probably come from his Cro-Magnon father. The little ivory goddess is called a Venus figurine. Similar statues have been found all over the world, but the oldest one dates only from about 20,000 B.C. The telepathic ability of Oomor's tribe is pure fantasy.

Yucky Food

Most people, apart from modern-day North Americans, eat creepy-crawly things (including insects, snails, and spiders) as part of their normal diet or as delicacies. These creatures are easy to catch and high in protein and fat, and they are eaten with enthusiasm by millions of people in Central and South America, Asia, and Africa. If you go to a good restaurant in France, Italy, Spain, Portugal, or Greece, you are likely to find snails on the menu. Most people also eat the brains, hearts, livers, kidneys, tongues, testicles, eyes, and intestines of various animals, as well as assorted algae, molds, and fungi. The blue cheese in blue cheese dressing contains mold; the mushrooms on your pizza are fungi.

I have eaten many of these things, including grilled grasshoppers in Oaxaca, huitlacoche (corn smut) in Mexico City, and snails in New York, Paris, Lisbon, Madrid, and Rome, and I enjoyed them all. People who like to try unfamiliar things have a lot more fun than those who don't.